The Ruby Moon

Trisha White Priebe
& Jerry B. Jenkins

SHILOH RUN PRESS
An Imprint of Barbour Publishing, Inc.

Cover Illustration: Scott Altmann
Cover Lettering: Kirk DouPonce

Published in association with The Blythe Daniel Agency, P.O. Box 64197, Colorado Springs, CO 80962-4197.

Published by Shiloh Run Press, an imprint of Barbour Publishing, Inc., P.O. Box 719, Uhrichsville, Ohio 44683, www.shilohrunpress.com

Our mission is to publish and distribute inspirational products offering exceptional value and biblical encouragement to the masses.

 Member of the
Evangelical Christian
Publishers Association

Printed in the United States of America.

Dedication

To Steven Joel Priebe
a.k.a. Henry

With special thanks to Kelly McIntosh, JoAnne Simmons,
and the rest of the editorial team, without whom this book
would not exist. Thank you for your time, talent, and tenacity.

chapter 1

The Underworld

"Hello?" Avery called, carefully stepping into the darkness.

Suddenly the air grew colder and the scent of wet earth grew stronger as the ground beneath her formed steps—cold, jagged stairs carved into stone—though she had no idea how many there were or where they led. She steadied herself and descended carefully, sliding each slippered foot over the edge and holding her breath.

Everything told her to turn around and go back to her room, to *safety*. She knew she shouldn't make this trip alone and without a candle.

But Avery had never preferred *safe*, and time was not on her side. She trusted her eyes would adjust to the darkness any minute so she could see what lay on this side of the mysterious door in the library before it was too late.

Footsteps?

She stopped and listened.

A rat, she decided. *No doubt the castle underbelly is full of them.*

She took another step. Why had it been so important to her mother to hide the key to this door in the back of a book with the words "This book must not be destroyed"?

With each step into the castle's frigid interior, the air became more pungent, like she was sinking into a sewer. She yanked her hand back from something slimy on the stone wall, her breath coming in cold puffs.

If she found where the stairs led, she might finally understand why she had been brought to the castle against her will and, more importantly, what had happened to her mother, father, and brother.

A silhouette.

Avery stopped, sure someone was moving toward her. She heard breathing.

"Who's there?" she called. "I demand you tell me your name."

Don't panic, she reminded herself. Too often her imagination got her into trouble. But just as she took another step, she felt someone in front of her.

She jumped back and shrieked.

Someone grabbed her wrist and clamped a hand over her mouth.

Icy and strong, it smelled of dead fish.

She felt hot breath as a woman whispered in her ear, "Go back where you came from and never come back. You are not welcome here."

Avery nodded vigorously, and when the figure melded back into the darkness, she turned and raced back up the stairs—tripping over the hem of her dress and bruising her shins on the stone steps—finally reaching the library door.

She would return to her side of the castle—for now.

The chaos inside and outside the castle had reached new heights as preparations for the king's grand Olympiad grew to a fevered pitch, raising excitement in the kids' quarters. The kitchen girls worked overtime making every imaginable delicacy. Rumor was, there would be enough sugared fruits to feed a tiny nation.

According to the scouts, brightly colored tents already dotted the landscape outdoors, and athletes in every possible sport trained on the grounds. When the scouts weren't busy monitoring the royals, they met in the kids' Great Room to reenact wrestling moves or practice their jousting skills with the king's discarded blades.

The girls volunteered to watch and critique, no experience necessary.

The next morning Avery arrived in the sitting room, flustered.

She was late for the morning cabinet meeting with Tuck, Kendrick, and Kate, but she wouldn't tell them she had discovered the key or that she had attempted to sneak into the castle's underbelly. She wouldn't admit that she tossed and turned in bed all night trying to figure out why the woman told her never to return. *What secrets does the underbelly hold?*

Tuck tossed grapes and caught them in his mouth, a swarm of Bronte's puppies running around his chair.

"You missed breakfast," he said, his mouth full.

Avery sat in her assigned spot. Picking up the agenda left at her place, she rolled her eyes.

Pointing to the list of topics, she said, "We're supposed to be discussing the king's pressing political agenda, but obviously he doesn't have one right now since he's busy throwing the world's greatest Olympiad. This meeting is a waste of time. I have other things to do." She stood to leave.

"Make no mistake," Kendrick shot back, "the Olympiad *is* the king's strategy."

"It's a series of games," she said.

Kendrick blew out a breath, and Avery knew she had

annoyed him. Adjusting his glasses and motioning for her to sit back down, Kendrick explained, "He knows his health is failing and his family's succession to the throne is at risk unless he produces an heir or establishes peace. Angelina isn't pregnant, so his only choice is to pursue goodwill with his enemies."

"What enemies?" Avery asked. "Inside or outside the kingdom?"

"Both. Plenty of people would love to see the throne pass to their own families. With word spreading that His Majesty is sick, people who want his power are already moving into the kingdom. Every day the scouts report new threats."

Kate said, "He's hosting the Olympiad to make everyone happy with him, but it won't happen."

"Agreed," Kendrick said, leaning back and tossing a grape to Tuck, who caught it in his mouth.

The boys broke into exaggerated cheers.

"I think this meeting is over," Avery said.

"Mark my words," Kendrick said, "the Olympiad is going to end badly."

Avery suspected her second trip to the castle's underbelly would also end badly, but next time she would take her jeweled dagger.

chapter 2

Kendrick's Secret

Avery slipped into the fragrant darkness of the pantry, bent until her knees met the cool tiled floor, and cranked open the slat to peer through the vent and check on the king.

Spying on him felt important, so she did it often, despite the risks.

As she suspected, he looked older and weaker than the last time she had checked. His thick silver hair was thinner, making his head look unusually large for his body. He had the hands of an old man, and he dozed when he should have been sifting through the important papers on his desk. He had a kingdom to run, and yet he couldn't even keep his eyes open.

Queen Angelina hurried in, replacing the silver mug on the king's desk with a second silver mug. She did this every morning, moving as quickly and quietly as a mouse.

Avery sat up, cranked the slat closed, and slipped back into the secret stairwell.

Returning to the kids' quarters, she found Kate sitting alone amid scraps of fabric, working on brightly colored silk flags for the Olympiad.

"Angelina is killing the king," Avery said bluntly.

Kate laughed. "First of all, how could you possibly know that? And second of all, how on earth could you prove it? Who would you tell, and why would anyone believe you? You could be sent to the gallows for simply suggesting it to the wrong person." Kate continued her sewing.

"Fine, but it doesn't change my opinion. Angelina doesn't seem the least bit upset that the king is ill, and the timing is wrong."

Kate didn't look up from her work. "The timing?"

"As soon as she married him, he grew visibly ill. Either she's contributing to his poor health, or she married him because she knew he was dying. Either way, I intend to prove she's involved."

Kate smiled, sewing the edge of a flag.

"I'm serious," Avery pressed.

"I'm sure you are, but why does it matter so much to you?"

"Because I believe Angelina is the reason we're here. If she gives birth to the king's heir and the king dies, it could mean destruction for all of us. The king may be the only reason we're still alive."

"He could also be the reason we're being held captive," Kate said. "How certain are you?"

Avery shrugged. "I'm sure a king is no match for the power of a determined woman."

Kate laughed. "Is that another theory you plan to prove?"

Avery nodded. "I'm not ready to face the king yet, but someday I will."

⌘

Later that evening, the thirteen-year-olds held a party in their meeting hall, wearing elaborate costumes and masks with gaudy embellishments obtained by the scouts after one of Angelina's recent festivities. The kitchen girls delivered platters of treats while the kids laughed and poked fun at each other late into the night.

Safe behind her elaborate gold mask with fabric roses, Avery decided to ask Kendrick the question she had been struggling with for days. He stood off to the side, leaning against the wall, holding up a wolf mask made of black feathers.

She was surprised he was holding a mask but not that he was alone. Avery took a deep breath and gathered her courage. Once she asked the question, she would never be able to take it back. He might laugh at her or worse, but she needed to know his answer more than she needed her next breath of air. She determinedly stepped over to him. Still behind her mask, she said quietly, "I need you to be honest with me."

He nodded.

Her throat tightened and she swallowed.

In that instant he lowered his mask, and she saw that he *wasn't Kendrick*!

Avery quickly spun and marched away, the strange boy calling after her.

She finally found Kendrick, sitting alone, reading. She considered forgetting the whole thing. She wasn't afraid he'd lie. She was afraid he might tell the truth and what that truth might be.

When he looked up at her, she knew it was now or never. She set down her mask.

Kendrick looked annoyed by the interruption, but he closed his book. "Well?"

"Your eyes," she said, barely above a whisper. "One is brown and the other is blue, just like the first queen."

It wasn't a question.

Kendrick's expression—as always—was blank.

Avery wondered whether he'd heard her. Or if he had but didn't understand the implication—which was itself an answer. At least he might not understand what she wanted to know, which might save her some embarrassment in the end.

He opened his book and stared at a page for a long moment. Avery was about to turn away when Kendrick slammed the book shut and stood, staring straight at her with those striking eyes.

"We can't talk about this here," he said.

She followed him into the stairwell and up the stairs until they arrived at a door with an X on it.

She grabbed Kendrick's arm. "We can't—"

But he pushed it open to reveal a tiny balcony under a sloping roof. He stepped out and hoisted himself onto the gable.

Closing the door, Avery followed, grateful for Kendrick's hand. She had climbed a thousand trees but never in a billowy dress.

They sat in silence under a net of stars, looking out over the Salt Sea and a cluster of houses glowing with golden candlelight.

It was strangely peaceful, like the roof of her castle tree house back home, only a heavy secret dangled between them.

Kendrick spoke quietly. "How long have you had it figured out?"

Avery turned to look at Kendrick in a new way. "You're—"

"The son of a king who doesn't even know my name," he said with a laugh. "Can you imagine how that feels?"

"No," she whispered. But of course, she *had* imagined how it felt to be the child of the king. What thirteen-year-old girl hadn't imagined a life better than her own? Now—ironically—she was living the life she had imagined and would give anything to return to the life she had taken for granted.

Avery could barely take it in. Kendrick was royalty. She leaned back on her elbows. "Start at the beginning."

Kendrick exhaled loudly, and Avery sensed that the walls Kendrick had built around himself were slowly crumbling. With the moon as their only witness, he began.

"I don't know my beginning," he said. "When I was eight or nine, I overheard the woman I believed was my mother telling a friend she was angry that the king did nothing to support me. My family was poor, and I was draining them of their resources."

"I'm sure you weren't—"

"I was a burden, and I always knew it. When I heard my mother say that, I finally understood why."

"And you never told your mother you knew the truth?"

Kendrick shook his head. "I was scared. I've learned since that the woman who raised me was a servant in the household of the first queen. She lived here in the castle. One of Queen Elizabeth's women sent me to live with my new family in one of the country houses on the other side of the Salt Sea."

"And you don't know why?"

He shook his head again and stared up at the sky.

"Legend says the king's only child died," Avery said. "Do you think the king even knows you were sent away? What if he doesn't know you're alive?"

Kendrick shrugged.

"You're still scared," Avery said.

"I'm *not* scared."

"Then what's stopping you? What if you are the heir the king wants? You could make him the happiest man on earth! He's sick and needs a son, and you *didn't die*!"

"But I will if Angelina finds me. It's a risk I'm not sure I want to take."

That sent a shiver up Avery's spine. "You don't believe there's *anything* you can do?"

Kendrick whispered, "I have never told my story until now."

"Don't worry. Your secret is safe with me."

"It may be," he answered, "but you aren't safer for knowing."

"Then why tell me?"

"Well, for one thing, you're the first one to figure it out. And you asked. Plus, you might be able to help."

Avery raised a brow. "How so?"

"Your mother has been right about everything else," Kendrick said. "The stories she told you when you were growing up included the underground colonies, the tunnels, and the evil queen. I'm certain she gave you the information we need to get out of here alive. You need to think hard about everything she ever told you. Even the details you feel are insignificant. She wouldn't have given you all this information and left out the most important clue."

Avery hoped he was right.

She, too, had suspected her mother had left bread crumbs of information for just this moment, but Avery couldn't for the life of her remember what they might be.

"I'll do my best," she said.

"I know you will. Once the king dies, the only thing I'll be good for is the gallows if Angelina knows where I am. You, too, if it comes out that you know my identity. We don't have much time."

They climbed down from the sloping roof and landed on the tiny balcony.

And they saw that the door stood open.

Someone had been listening!

chapter 3

Digging Graves

Keeping her promise to Kendrick, Avery plumbed her memories of her mother's stories while pacing the stairwell or staring absently at her book in the sitting room or while bartering with other thirteen-year-olds in the makeshift shop.

She rehearsed everything she could remember while eating with Kate. At night she dreamed of conversations with her mother and relived the nights she curled up beside her to listen to the stories of her past while scented raindrops pelted the paper-thin windows of their tiny cottage.

The only result of all this effort was that Avery missed her mother even more.

She dreaded having to tell Kendrick she had nothing helpful to offer him. He would be rightfully annoyed.

⌘

Kate's sewing room looked like a market stall with its colorful bolts of fabric stacked side by side. Avery loved to sneak upstairs and watch her friend work.

"What's on your mind?" Kate asked without looking up, sticking pins into freshly cut fabric.

Avery smiled, her lip quivering. "It's about your grandmother."

Kate set down her tools and looked up. "Go on."

"After she took Henry and me from the woods, she must have instructed someone to take my brother somewhere—another village, maybe, or somewhere here in the castle?"

Kate looked away. Avery wondered if this conversation came too soon after the old woman's death.

Finally Kate said, "If you're asking me where Henry is, I don't know."

"But you must!" Avery blurted. "You know everything else about the inner workings of the court, and your grandmother is the reason—" Sleepless nights had made her emotional. She would get nowhere blaming Kate's grandmother.

Kate nodded and said quietly, "You should spend time in the chapel."

Avery smiled. Her mother always gave her the same advice when she was struggling with something. *"You will find the answers to your most important questions there."*

But Avery didn't find her answers in the chapel, especially the ornate one upstairs in the castle, no matter how often she went. She preferred immediate answers—with audible replies.

She wished her mother—and Kate—would offer more useful advice.

⸎

At the end of each day, the scouts updated the cabinet.

They met in the sitting room off the kids' dining room, where Bronte and her litter of quickly growing pups scratched the floor and nipped at each other's ears while the council talked of serious matters.

In addition to the colorful tents near the king's gardens, tonight two of the scouts claimed to have laid eyes on the largest stadium they had ever seen, being built on the east end of the royal land. They used terms like *magnificent* and *brilliant* and *astounding*—words larger than their usual vocabulary.

Avery itched to get out and see it.

"It will house the biggest events of the Olympiad," one of the scouts explained. "His Majesty has hired the best workers to build it, sparing no expense."

"And the king himself visits every day to make sure the builders are on target," the second cut in. "Rumor is, he's willing to bankrupt the realm to make sure everyone at these games is the happiest they've ever been."

Avery noticed what the scouts left unsaid.

No one is allowed to be unhappy.

"Or what?" she mumbled.

"Appearances mean everything to this king," Kendrick whispered beside her while the scouts continued talking. "He doesn't care if you truly are happy, so long as you *look* like you are." He paused then whispered, "Have you thought of anything new from your mother's stories yet?"

Avery shook her head. Kendrick exhaled loudly.

"Anything else?" Tuck asked the scouts.

They looked at each other and seemed to hesitate.

"There is one more thing," one said. "The king is still searching for a runner to represent the crown in the half-mile race. It's eight laps of 110 yards each, and the winner receives a private audience with the king."

Avery sat a little straighter and looked from member to member of the council.

"Won't anyone volunteer?" Tuck asked.

The scouts shook their heads. "His Majesty believes victory at the Olympiad will signal God's favor on his reign," one said. "So even the most competent runners are refusing, for fear the opposite will prove God's displeasure."

Tuck thanked the scouts and dismissed them.

Avery didn't hesitate. "I can run. I'm fast. And I know how to endure distances like that."

She hoped she sounded more casual than she felt, because a half-mile run was a killer—long enough to exhaust a person but too short to allow you to slack off and pace yourself without losing. Still, her heart kicked up the way it did when an idea energized her.

This could be my chance to meet the king!

But Tuck had already moved on to other matters.

Avery couldn't sleep. She lay there rolling questions over in her mind.

How did it benefit the royal family to pretend the king's son died?

What if the king never knew his son lived?

Could Kendrick be the answer to our problems?

The answers could mean freedom or death. She needed to know which.

"You're thinking about your brother, aren't you?" Kate asked.

Avery rolled over and shrugged.

"I've been thinking about what you said," Kate continued. "And you're right, my grandmother probably did know what happened to Henry, but she never told me. Do you remember anything about your conversation with her?"

"She said she didn't want to have to dig another grave." Hot tears gathered in Avery's eyes.

Kate sat up, threw off her blanket, and moved to sit on the edge of Avery's mattress. "My grandmother wouldn't have killed your brother," she said. "It was her job to bury the children of royals who died in the womb or shortly after birth. More than once my grandmother had to dig a grave for a mourning mother. She often told me she never wanted to see another dead child. I'm sure—wherever Henry is right now—he is alive and well."

Avery nodded. She wanted to believe it. She also wanted to believe she would find him someday.

She drifted to sleep a few minutes later with the hope that Henry lived.

chapter 4

Disappearance

Kate looked unusually somber at breakfast, stabbing a fork into her breakfast potatoes.

Avery wondered if she had hurt her with the questions about her grandmother. She hadn't intended to; she only wanted answers. She owed it to Kendrick to turn over every stone of her memory. She was just summoning the courage to apologize when Kate said quietly, "Do not go back to the tunnels."

Kate was so direct Avery was startled.

"I know you're fascinated with the underworld," Kate continued, unflinching, "but don't be. Nothing good happens there."

"Who told you I went into the tunnels?"

"Just listen for once, and don't go down there. You aren't welcome."

The familiar words gave Avery a chill, but she wasn't about to make a promise she couldn't keep. She was already planning her next trip, better prepared this time with a candle, matches, and a blade. But she was going.

"Don't do it," Kate said. "Promise me—no more exploring."

"Not without a good reason," Avery said evenly.

"My grandmother went into the tunnels the day she died," Kate pushed. "I believe she discovered something she wasn't meant to find."

"Well, that may be," Avery said, "but I—"

Tuck stood on his chair at the center of the table and called for everyone's attention. The usual scraping of silverware against tin plates stopped.

"The king has been searching for the fastest half-miler in the realm for the Olympiad, and it appears he need look no further."

Tuck caught Avery's gaze, and she smiled. The table broke into animated conversation. The kids hadn't had anything to be this excited about since the royal wedding.

Tuck continued, "Of course, the king has no idea a thirteen-year-old will run the race, but I believe he'll be pleased. *We* play to win!"

The kids cheered.

"Would you like to know who will represent us?"

More cheers. Avery pushed back her chair.

"Thomas, please stand!"

Avery froze, staring.

A gangly, red-faced, shaggy-haired boy rose to a roar of shouts and the occasional whoop.

Avery didn't know Thomas, but she was certain she could outrun him. She outran everyone back home—boys included, and this guy didn't look like anything special. It had taken him a snail's age to simply push back his chair and stand.

When he swept his hair aside, his wrist showed a crisscrossed web of scars. Everything about him set her nerves on edge.

"Don't be jealous," Kate said when everyone resumed eating. "He'll have a lot of pressure on his shoulders. If the king believes victory signals God's favor, the athletes compete at the risk of their lives. Better not to run and live than to lose and die."

"I'm not jealous," Avery said, slicing into her meat with extra vigor, but her voice squeaked, and Kate smiled.

In truth, Avery wanted to run to more than just prove she could win. She wanted that audience with the king so she could tell him about Kendrick. She had already imagined the whole scenario, complete with the curtsy and the life-changing words, "Your son is alive!"

Of course that would be a colossal risk in itself. The king could kill her on the spot if it was a secret he wanted sealed. But if it proved to be news he welcomed, he might grant her freedom. She envisioned a grateful king returning the favor of helping her find her family.

How will I ever know for sure if I don't talk to him?

And how will I ever talk to him if I don't run the race?

A scout appeared, wildly beckoning Kate and Avery. "Quickly!" he said. "You're needed in the kitchen!"

⚭

One of the kitchen girls hadn't shown up to help with breakfast, and the others were a mess of gossip and fear. Their eyes and noses were red as they spilled the details. "We've looked everywhere!" one said.

"We assumed she overslept," another explained, "but she's nowhere to be found. We're afraid something terrible has happened."

This signaled a chorus of cries from the rest.

"It's too early to panic," Kate said, throwing a glance at Avery. "Sometimes people like to explore, even when it isn't in their best interest."

Avery called over the din, "She may be back by noon with a good explanation. Sometimes people explore for all the right reasons. Let's wait and see."

⁓∞⁓

When noon came with no sign of the missing girl, word spread like wildfire. Comparisons were made to Edward and his sudden disappearance. Questions floated around the lunch table.

Where could she have gone? What if she's in danger? Could she have left by choice?

Things only grew worse the next morning when a boy with the courage of a housefly went missing from his bed. By supper a third child had disappeared.

"What's happening?" Avery whispered.

Kate, in a rare moment of vulnerability, looked as frightened as the rest of the thirteen-year-olds. "I don't know," she said, "and I have a feeling I don't want to know."

Who would be next?

chapter 5

Lost

That kids were snatched from their beds in the night and whisked off to who-knows-where was chilling, but that they were also grabbed midday was doubly terrifying. The cabinet began performing roll calls before every meal.

Each time, someone was gone.

All excitement about the Olympiad had vanished with the missing kids.

The council questioned each missing kid's friends and work partners.

Was he happy?

Had she been acting strange before she disappeared?

Did you notice anything unusual?

Each interview raised more questions than answers.

"This may sound heartless, Avery," Kate whispered from her bed one night, "but not only are our friends disappearing, but our workload is getting harder. We won't be able to keep up if we lose any more."

"That *is* heartless, Kate. I'm worried about who'll be next. It could be any of us."

"The problem is," Kate continued, "if we can't keep up with our workload, the few adults who know about our existence in the castle will have no reason to keep our secret."

The girls lay back against their pillows, Avery too nervous to go to sleep and alert to every sound. Even with scouts posted outside the bunkroom door around the clock, how could anyone feel safe?

That question was answered in the morning when Thomas—the runner—didn't show up to breakfast. He was often late. But after one of the other boys went to look for him and came back eerily white and shaken, everyone knew.

The dining room erupted in a frenzy.

Tuck caught Avery's eye from across the table. "Meeting after breakfast," he mouthed.

Kendrick, Kate, and Avery sat in the sitting room as Tuck paced.

Avery had seen Tuck this upset only the day she had

returned to the castle after sneaking back to her family home. He was inconsolable. "We've got to fix this!"

"How can the scouts have seen nothing?" Avery said. "People can't disappear into thin air. Someone isn't talking."

"How do we make them talk?" Kendrick asked.

"We don't," Kate said. "We begin with what we know."

"We're disappearing the same way we all arrived," Kendrick said.

"Not exactly," Avery said. "Sorry to be blunt, Kate, but obviously your grandmother isn't involved."

"What I mean," Kendrick continued, "is there appears to be no pattern. The missing seem to have nothing in common."

"We only *assume* they're being snatched," Avery said. "What if they're leaving because they've found a way out? Leaving by choice?"

"Why wouldn't they share the news with their closest friends? And where would they go?" Kate asked. "It's not like most of us have homes to return to, and it's the wrong time of year to sleep outdoors."

Tuck stopped. "We need to move," he said. "We've got to find a place to relocate before the next person is grabbed. At the very least, relocating might buy us time to learn what's happening."

"Where could we possibly go that would be large enough to hide everyone?" Kendrick asked.

Avery shot Kate a knowing glance.

She would go back to the tunnels tonight with or without Kate's approval.

⬥

Avery intended her second trip into the tunnels to be brief. She wanted to approach Tuck with the idea of moving, but she needed more information. He would ask where they would sleep, eat, meet, and work.

She hadn't considered getting lost.

Yet, thirty minutes into her trip, the maze of interconnecting chambers broken by giant columns dizzied her. With only a candle to guide her, the catacomb of blown-out rooms overwhelmed. The space was enough to house an underground city. But the longer she walked and the deeper she traveled into the castle's underbelly, the more certain she felt she had gotten in over her head.

Armed with a pocket of matches and her jeweled dagger, she moved silently through the space, wondering how many eyes watched her from the deep shadows.

She turned a corner and realized she had already seen

this part of the tunnel.

In fact, twice—maybe three times.

She had heard the tunnels were a death trap to anyone incapable of figuring them out. It was the castle's hideous joke on lawless men who hid in its subterranean shadows to avoid the dungeon or the chopping block.

Bending, she quickly dragged her fingers through the mysterious sludge coating the floor, drew an X on the wall, and picked up her pace.

Avery saw the same X again a few minutes later and slumped against the wall.

Tears stung as she rested her head in her arms. She smelled dead fish and heard a voice she recognized immediately. "I told you never to come back here again."

Avery whipped around in time to see the dim light of a waning torch. She pushed herself up and backed away from the voice, reaching for the dagger in her pocket.

The voice continued, "Go straight until you reach a fork. Then left until you see the X that leads to the stairs. And *don't come back*. I know who you are. You aren't safe here."

Avery turned and ran, relief sweeping over her when she reached the library and let herself back inside. She had been gone much longer than she intended.

She wouldn't make that mistake again.

chapter 6

A Terrible Idea

Girls huddled in the bunkroom, wailing. Avery knew immediately someone else was missing, but who?

She approached a group of girls, frantically searching for Kate. "What happened? Who's missing?"

A great cry went up as Kate raced across the room and grabbed Avery, shaking her. Kate's voice quavered with rage. "Where have you been, Avery?"

Confused by the startled expressions, Avery finally comprehended what had caused the upset. *I missed supper. I missed roll call. I wasn't in my room.*

"I'm sorry," she said quietly. "I lost track of time."

"You were *gone!*" a girl wailed.

"So sorry," Avery said, louder now, realizing everyone thought she had been swallowed by that mysterious hole everyone seemed to be falling into one by one. She was overcome that girls who had never spoken to her had been mourning her demise and were now celebrating her appearance.

Grief makes best friends of strangers.

Within moments, the crisis had passed and the girls had moved on to other things.

"Where were you?" Kate demanded.

"You know where, and don't start with me. I had no choice. You heard what Tuck said about moving. You know the tunnels are a good choice—maybe even our *only* choice."

"It's my *job* to keep you safe," Kate said.

"Says who?"

Kate looked away and her tone softened. "Especially right now, you need to follow orders. Please, for me, stay out of the tunnels."

◦❧◦

Tuck wanted Avery to join him in the sitting room after supper, and she knew that couldn't mean good news. The twinkle was gone from his eyes, and she hadn't seen him smile since the thirteen-year-olds started disappearing. She just hoped Kate hadn't told him where she'd been.

He'll take her side for sure. Everyone always does.

In the corner of the sitting room, she found Tuck, Kendrick, Kate, and a scout she didn't know. Tuck motioned for her to sit. "We have a problem."

"Only one?" Kendrick muttered.

"As you know," Tuck continued, "Thomas was to run in the Olympiad half mile. We have no idea if he'll be found in time."

"The scouts want you to run," Kate blurted. "It's a terrible idea."

Tuck nodded. "Terrible."

Avery looked to Kendrick, who shrugged and turned away.

"We hope Thomas will be found," the scout said, "but we need a backup. The king will be furious if no one represents the kingdom. We were told to produce a runner, and if we don't, there will be no mercy."

Everyone looked grave.

Kendrick said, "The king doesn't give second chances, Avery. Whoever runs must win."

"You think I can't?"

No one looked her in the eye.

"What do you think, Tuck? Do you believe I can win?"

Tuck didn't respond.

"You're the only one willing to try," the scout said. "You could get out of the castle a bit. See the Olympiad up close, visit the tents."

Avery's friends shook their heads.

"If something happened to you. . . ," Tuck said.

"I'll do it," Avery said, a little too loudly.

I'll prove I can do something right.

⚜

In bed that night, Avery began to doubt her decision.

Who might her competition be? Whoever it was, they had likely been training for months while she had been cooped up letting her muscles shrivel and grow weak.

Why am I so impulsive? What have I agreed to?

This wouldn't be one of her races back home on a bright, cold morning where the winner received the praises of her friends. The outcome of this race could mean the difference between freedom and the tower, life and death.

Unable to sleep, she dressed and went to the Great Room the kids used for midnight court. She ran as quickly as she could from one side of the room to the other until she was exhausted. She looked silly, but she didn't care. It felt good to fill her lungs again and feel the ground fly beneath her bare feet—even if it was marble instead of dirt. Avery was not ready for a half mile, but if she ran each night while her friends slept—also on the stairs and through the halls—maybe she would be.

A shift in the shadows just outside the room caught her eye.

She needed to get back to her mattress before anyone worried.

Avery lay staring at the ceiling and decided, regardless how the race ended, she owed it to her friends to tell them they had a safer place to live right beneath them. If it was the last thing she did, she would ensure their safe passage to the tunnels.

She *needed* to go back underground, and she needed someone to go with her.

chapter 7

Taking Kate

Avery cautiously approached the storage room where each afternoon Kate organized the shipment of castle castoffs the scouts delivered by the trunk load. With the Olympiad fast approaching, the castle was in pandemonium, with artisans making new clothes and fashioning new jewelry, so castoffs were plentiful. Most wound up in the kids' store, where the thirteen-year-olds bought and sold with marbles.

"I need you to come with me," Avery said.

Kate looked up from sorting a box of furs. "Where?"

Avery paused, summoning her courage. "To explore the tunnels."

Kate started to protest, but Avery put up a hand. "If Tuck is serious about moving us, the tunnels could be our only option. I just need one more visit and someone to go with me who's— I know you told me not to go back and I know it's not safe, but it's not safe staying on this side of the castle either. I'd rather get in trouble trying to find a solution than be snatched while doing nothing. I know this isn't a game."

"But it *is*," Kate said. "We just have to prove ourselves better at playing it. Let's go!"

⚮

Avery and Kate huddled as they moved down the stone steps—the candle between them sending eerie shadows dancing ahead. Avery felt guilty that she hadn't told Kate about the woman who had grabbed her arm or that she had gotten lost on her second trip.

But how many secrets is Kate keeping from me?

They reached a landing where a dank passageway formed what appeared to be an endless tunnel ahead. Tiny room-like alcoves jutted from the main passage. Some were large, like sitting rooms, capable of holding midnight court for all the thirteen-year-olds. Others were small and could serve as tiny bedchambers or washrooms. Avery whispered these ideas as they walked.

The deeper they moved into the tunnels, the more torches they found perched on random sconces. Water seemed to drip everywhere, creating puddles they tried to avoid, and the backs of their dresses dragged through the sludgy pools. "We'd have to get used to that infernal dripping noise," Kate said. "It's constant."

"We could hope it would eventually fade into the background," Avery said.

But she knew that was unlikely.

The deeper in they ventured, the more people they found—clusters of hungry-looking, agitated characters who looked none too pleased with two well-dressed girls invading their territory. Avery hadn't seen them on her previous visits and suspected the tunnels were filled with more people restless for revenge.

"What was that?" Avery asked at groaning off to the side.

"I don't think we want to know," Kate said. "Keep walking."

Avery saw movement up ahead and thrust the candle forward. A woman with fierce eyes sat with a group of children huddled around her, a crying baby pressed to her heart. She quickly pulled a hood over her face and slunk back from the light.

"Wonder what she's afraid of," Avery whispered.

"Who knows what she might've done?" Kate said. "She's not likely a friend of the castle. They call this the underworld for a reason. Some of the castle's greatest enemies disappeared down here. Which is why moving down here may not be such a good idea."

"What choice do we have? Stay upstairs until someone snatches us, or move down here and take our chances."

∞

Despite small bunches of people in various alcoves, there appeared to be plenty of room for the kids to live and conduct their business. Large passages remained unoccupied.

They approached a shady-looking group of men and Avery whispered, "Should we go back?"

"We've made it this far," Kate said. "Let's keep moving."

Avery's eyes darted as she edged past the men, and she clung tight to Kate. The men called out salty comments, but Avery focused on gathering information to make a strong case to Tuck. She was about to finish and head back upstairs when she heard a voice—unmistakable in tone— and stopped.

"Sounds like my mother," Avery whispered.

Kate tugged her toward the door. "Can't be."

But even as they walked, Avery noticed the odd way Kate looked over her shoulder on their way out.

chapter 8

Last One Standing

Despite the growing number of empty chairs at the thirteen-year-olds' breakfast table, the dining room was a swirl of excitement on the opening day of the Olympiad. The kids made their predictions and wagered their chores. The scouts were given strict instructions to report back often with whatever details they could collect.

For the moment, all seemed normal again.

Avery picked at her food, frustrated not to be outside. She wanted so badly to know if anyone from home was in the crowd. Rumor had it, the Salt Sea was filled to the brim with covered boats carrying men, women, and children from throughout the realm to watch and participate in the tournaments.

"I *need* to be out there," Avery said.

"Don't even think about it," Kate said, laughing.

But, of course, Avery could do nothing *but* think about it. When everyone else was finished and gone and the kitchen crew was clearing the table, Avery still sat there, resting her head against her fist, imagining ways she might escape for the day.

She sensed someone watching her and turned to see Kendrick. "Come with me," he said.

Avery was in no mood to talk about his royal blood or the lack of details she could remember from her mother's stories, but she remembered the day he had followed her to the library, trusting her without question.

Plus, she needed a good distraction.

Down the stairs they went and through a set of doors until they arrived at a cellar that jutted off on ground level. A door to the outside world was bolted with a heavy gold chain and lock, and Avery wondered if Kendrick had plans to pick it.

But how?

He put his ear against the door, but Avery could plainly hear the din of voices and the clattering of carts. The taste of freedom just out of reach.

"What are we doing?" she whispered.

"Just wait," Kendrick said, clearly annoyed.

After what seemed an eternity, suddenly the noise on the other side of the door stopped.

Kendrick put a finger to his lips.

A single brass instrument Avery could not identify played a sweet, perfect melody that wafted over the grounds, slipped under the door, and filled the room.

Avery put a hand to her mouth. *My song—the opening ceremony of the Olympiad.*

In all the activity and commotion, Avery had long forgotten she had written the opening song at the king's request. Kendrick alone had remembered.

In tears, eyes closed, she listened.

She had embellished the tune her parents had created and made it appropriate for the occasion. Maybe, just maybe, if her father came within earshot of the Olympiad, he would recognize the song and know where to find her.

⚭

The kids spent the afternoon and early evening rehearsing the news that had wound its way through the castle. Their favorite update? . . . The king had released doves at the opening ceremony—so many that the birds made an uproarious mess on the heads of commoners and noblemen alike. This story brought rounds of repetition and laughter, complete with hand gestures and sound effects. No matter how many times it was repeated, it never got old.

For the moment at least, the thirteen-year-olds had something to smile about, despite the fact two more of their friends had disappeared since breakfast. The group was considerably smaller, and everyone couldn't help but wonder whether he or she might be next. They started to congregate in groups more often than not.

Safety in numbers.

⚬∞⚬

Avery and Kendrick met again on the edge of the roof that overlooked the water in the starlight.

Dozens of boats bobbed on the slapping sea, bearing witness to the extraordinary effort the king was making to preserve his legacy.

Sitting among the spires and peaked rooftops of the castle, Avery and Kendrick talked about the secret they shared and what they thought was happening to the kids who disappeared.

"There are now more of us missing than remaining," Kendrick said, reviewing the names on his list.

"We've got to link the missing with *when* they vanished," Avery said. "There has to be some connection. We just have to find it."

Kendrick quickly looked away.

"What are you not telling me?" she asked.

He sighed heavily. "It's a long shot, but they do have something in common."

It seemed an eternity before he continued.

"None of those missing pose a threat to the queen," he said.

Avery narrowed her gaze. "I don't understand."

"What if the thirteen-year-olds are being released once someone officially clears them of any succession to the throne?"

"A literal reversal of how we were brought here?"

"Right," Kendrick said. "Suppose Angelina orchestrated our capture, looking for the king's heir. Any thirteen-year-old without royal blood is merely her pawn—disposable."

"All of us but you, you mean."

Kendrick nodded.

Avery said quietly, "So this means—"

"I live in constant danger. Once the group is whittled down, I'll be the last one standing."

"It's time to tell Tuck and Kate," Avery said.

Kendrick shook his head. "Telling them puts them in danger, too."

Just then a fat, black raven landed beside them and let out a dreadful squawk that made Avery and Kendrick scramble inside.

chapter 9

The Gallows

Tuck's voice was low. "You went *where?*"

"You heard me," Avery said. "It's bad enough waking up every morning to the news that another of us has disappeared. I can't stand the thought that someday it might be you, Kate, or Kendrick. You said we needed to find somewhere to move to, so I did."

"You shouldn't have gone alone! It's dangerous down there."

"Kate went with me."

Tuck gave her a look.

Not the right answer.

"Fine. I should have told you I was going. I'm sorry. But you should at least consider it. There's plenty of space, and we could move quickly."

Tuck let out a sigh and rubbed his hands over his face. "But is it safe?"

"Of course not. But it has to be safer than staying here

right now, wouldn't you agree?"

Tuck had never looked so tired to her before. His bright, fierce eyes were clouded, and his shoulders slumped like an old man's.

"It might work in an emergency," he said. "Good work, I guess."

Avery turned to leave.

"Wait," Tuck said, "one more thing. I don't want you to run tomorrow."

"I know. You don't think I can win."

"Listen, Avery. Already three different adults who lost their events have disappeared. Our scouts have no idea what happened to them."

"What do *you* think happened to them?"

Tuck slid a finger across his throat.

"But the ones who win are granted private audiences with the king. It's a chance I need to take. I've been training, and I'm ready."

Avery expected Tuck to argue, *wanted* him to argue. She wasn't sure she wanted to run after all, but backing out now would make her look like a coward. And after all the mistakes she'd made in the castle, she wanted to prove herself.

Tuck nodded and turned toward the door.

Avery called after him, "Tuck, I need your support!"

But he didn't look back.

⚬∞⚬

Avery spent the day running in the private stairwell and stretching in the hall the kids used for midnight court. She envisioned herself at the starting line in the Olympiad, and her heart beat like a horse thundering down a track. This would be the biggest risk she had ever taken.

Losing was not an option.

Ilsa appeared. "Come with me. There's something you need to see," she said. Avery knew better than to go, but she didn't have a reason to refuse. They made their way near the sewing room to a chamber in which Avery had never been.

Ilsa pulled the curtain back from a large window that overlooked part of the castle grounds, and revealed a group of men building a wood stage with a tall frame and metal fittings. Avery heard the hammering like the beating of a drum and the hiss of flame against metal. A noose had been fastened at the end of a thick rope tied to the crossbeam.

"Anyone who doesn't represent the kingdom well in the Olympiad," Ilsa said, "or anyone who brings shame on the king, gets a personal tour of these gallows." She let the curtain fall back into place and chirped, "Best of luck."

As Ilsa turned to leave, Avery said, "Why do you hate me? Have I done something so bad we can't work things out?"

Ilsa turned and held her gaze, and Avery couldn't discern her look. *Sadness? Fear? Loneliness?*

Sometimes the meanest people are hurting the most.

Their eyes locked, and Avery remembered what her mother had always quoted from the Bible. *"Bless them that curse you, and pray for them which despitefully use you."*

"You win," Avery said, and she moved past Ilsa and into the stairwell.

With only hours until the race, she couldn't dwell on losing.

Too much was at stake.

chapter 10

Risk

On what she knew could be the last morning of her life, Avery rose before dawn and ate in silence. If she did die today, her greatest regret would be not seeing her family one last time.

She returned to the bunkroom where Kate presented her with a pair of dark trousers, a long-sleeved shirt, and a pair of boots.

"Don't roll up your sleeves," Kate said solemnly, "or the star on your wrist will show. Bounty hunters will be watching for it."

Avery felt strange replacing her heavy dress and glittering slippers, but of course she would slip out of the boots and run the race barefoot—the way she liked to run at home.

Kate had disappeared while she was changing, but stepping into the hall, Avery ran into Tuck—pacing, hands clasped behind his back, worry etching his face.

"What do you think?" Avery asked, offering an exaggerated curtsy.

He was clearly not amused. "I think I may never see you again."

Avery sighed. "You don't need to remind me you're against this. It's too late to change my mind."

"It's *not* too late," he whispered, pleading with his eyes. "But you do have my support, and you always will." He stepped closer. "Promise me you'll win. You've got to!"

Alarmed by the terror in his eyes, Avery couldn't stay mad at him. All traces of his trademark confidence were gone.

"Of course," she said, feigning her best smile. She was relieved to see Kate approaching, so she could escape this awkward exchange.

As she turned to leave, Tuck said, "You were born to lead. Go be a leader."

∽∞∾

Back in the bunkroom, Avery sat on a stool while Kate worked silently, straightening Avery's hair—pinning each lock so it appeared short rather than long and unruly. Kate used more force each time she pressed a pin against Avery's head, making her wince.

"Is everything all right?" Avery finally asked, turning to

face her. "My scalp would like to make peace."

Kate stopped and pressed her lips together. Finally she said, "Anything could happen today. The king won't accept second place."

"You, too? Nobody thinks I can win. But I *will*."

Kate sighed. "I've always admired your confidence, but there's a fine line between conviction and stupidity. You never should have agreed to run."

She added more pins to Avery's hair, more gently now.

"The king can't know you're thirteen, or even that you're a girl," Kate continued, her voice cracking. "We can't help you if something happens. You're on your *own*."

Tears filled Avery's eyes as she realized how much her friends cared. Not that long ago they were strangers trying to figure out why they had been captured and hauled to the castle. Now they were family.

Avery turned to face Kate. "I *won't* lose," she said. "I can't. I'm running for you, for all of us, for our brothers and sisters—for an audience with the king. I'm running to get us out of here."

Kate's smile did not reach her eyes. "I know you are, and I love you for it, but you need to run for *you*. I want you back here tonight, safe and sound." She reached for a stray strand of hair, but Avery caught her hand and held it.

"You're my friend, Kate. Please, let's talk about something else—something happier." She ran her thumb over the ruby ring that had become a fixture on Kate's finger. "Tell me about this. It's beautiful."

"It belonged to my grandmother. It's a locket." Kate slipped it off, opened it, and showed Avery the tiny piece of rolled parchment inside. "She wrote me this message, but I'll never show anyone what it says."

As Kate replaced the message and clamped the ring closed, Avery wondered if her own ruby flower necklace had also been a locket. And if so, did it have a message inside? How she wished she could hold it one more time, especially today.

In a final effort to make Avery look as much like a boy as possible, Kate affixed a light cap to her head and pulled it low over her brow. She tucked the final stray strands of Avery's hair underneath and pinned the cap in place.

"Don't let anyone talk you into running without the cap."

Avery stood and pulled Kate into a hug, whispering, "I *won't* lose."

chapter 11

Henry

The springlike day smelled of musk and citrus with a tang of salt also heavy in the air.

Avery was as excited as she was scared as she surveyed the tents and made her way through the festivities.

The Olympiad was like nothing she had ever witnessed.

One persistent merchant sang loudly and off-key as he sold marzipan cakes to enthusiastic children. Another tilted his head back and spouted a flame from his mouth to rousing applause from a spellbound audience. A third hawked tickets to see his menagerie of exotic animals—rumored to be saber-toothed tigers and pure white lions—caged behind the castle. Every once in a while a random roar sent an unsuspecting Olympiad observer running.

A fourth, slightly subtler salesman caught Avery's eye. He peddled the ability to leave the past behind.

For a few copper coins, the handsome young huckster asked what guilt a person carried and wrote it on a tiny piece of parchment. He then attached the parchment to a small paper lantern, set it afire, and released it into the atmosphere, supposedly carrying the guilt of the deed with it.

"You'll never lose a wink of sleep again!" he'd say, his eyes twinkling.

Clever, Avery decided, because he now knew the deepest secrets of the townspeople and could make a few more coins via blackmail or by selling the secrets to the man who printed the daily bulletin.

In search of something to eat, Avery entered a crowded tent and through the din heard a voice bright and familiar as any she knew. "Is that apple sausage?" a young boy asked.

She whirled to see him at a distance from behind, but Avery recognized immediately the little brother she had left in the woods. *Henry.* He was a little taller and a tad leaner, but his light brown hair and pudgy hands were a giveaway.

She moved quickly—knocking into people, determined not to take her eyes off of him. He stood with a woman Avery didn't recognize but to her relief looked refined and kind. The woman stopped to talk to someone, and Avery dropped to her knees behind the child.

"Henry," she whispered and, with a hand on each shoulder, spun him around.

He had a sweet face, a button nose, and an easy smile. But he was not Henry.

"Sorry," she said, struggling to her feet and feeling herself flush from her neck to her hairline as pinpricks filled her head and clouded her vision. The boy stepped back, and the woman glared at her and drew him close.

"So sorry," Avery said, "I was mistaken." And she quickly moved into the crowd again. She dared not attract too much attention, a girl, after all, in boys' clothing.

Her heart aching, she slipped into the first tent she saw, anxious for a distraction.

The large tent was dominated by a gigantic chandelier and a huge table surrounded by velvet-covered chairs. Well-dressed men and women scurried about, carrying platters of food and drink to several other tables, each graced by elaborate candelabras at either end, at least a dozen candles glowing in every one. Avery couldn't help but covet a tenth of the excess lighting for herself and her peers.

Guards stood sentinel near the entrances.

And she suddenly understood.

This is the king's tent.

His Majesty was, no doubt, observing any of the vast number of tournaments happening simultaneously throughout the castle grounds. She wondered if this would be where she might finally encounter him if she won the race.

"You must be a runner!" a buoyant voice said from behind her. "Not enough meat on those bones to be a boxer!"

Avery turned to nod and recognized one of the king's advisers she had seen from observing the royal study through the kitchen floor. He laughed as if he had just told the funniest joke ever.

Avery pulled her cap a little lower.

"Cheer up, boy!" the adviser said, clapping her on the back. "It'll be over before you know it. Half a dozen races will be run on that track today. And I'll let you in on a little secret. Win and you'll be given a greater reward than you could possibly dream of in that little head of yours." He poked her in the temple, and she winced. "Our king loves a winner!"

He laughed and moved on, grabbing a chicken drumstick off a servant's platter and tossing it to Avery. She caught it and nodded a thank-you before biting into it.

In truth, Avery had been thinking of little other than

the opportunity to talk to the king. Because the race time was near, she limited herself to the one chicken leg and went in search of the stadium. She couldn't be late.

After a long walk through teeming crowds, Avery crested a hill and came face-to-face with the arena built for the Olympiad. Its magnitude and majesty stunned her.

She trembled and her knees went weak.

chapter 12

The Race

A grand oval building of marble rose before her, boasting three levels of stands supported by massive round pillars and covered by silk awnings to protect spectators from the sun.

Her legs froze, and she considered running the opposite direction.

But then she pictured the faces of those she loved and she pressed forward.

As she entered the arena, her stomach tightened with each step.

She half expected the track to be paved in gold, but just like the king, the exterior of this stadium was much more impressive than the interior. She soon realized her race would take place on little more than an enormous rectangle of cleared ground.

As the twelve competitors began gathering, the crowd roared.

The sea of faces made Avery wish she was oblivious to

how many people were watching. Only when someone called for the runners to take their places did Avery assess her competition for the first time.

None looked like eager recruits.

She would run against a crop of lanky boys who, no doubt, felt the pressure to impress their own masters. One—tall and gangly with a shaved head—looked more uncomfortable than the rest. He bit his lower lip and shook.

He looked familiar, and she briefly caught his eye, but Avery couldn't place him.

Like the rest, he didn't look happy.

A few peeled off their shirts and tossed them aside. Avery's shirt and cap would draw additional attention she didn't need. But so would winning. She shed only her boots and socks.

"To your marks!" a man called. Avery wriggled her way to the center. "Eight laps," he continued, "one half mile," pacing before them and droning a list of rules.

Avery whispered a prayer and waited. And the boy she thought she recognized wiped his brow, exposing a wrist crisscrossed with scars.

Thomas. The shaggy hair had been shaved to the scalp, but it was him.

At a trumpet blast, the runners exploded. For the first lap they ran shoulder to shoulder, but soon Avery and three others separated themselves from the rest. Thomas's long, loping stride appeared effortless and gave him a comfortable lead near the end of lap two.

Avery's throat tightened as she realized Thomas would be difficult—if not impossible—to catch. She thought of her parents and her brother, and though adrenaline surged through her, by lap three Thomas had put even more distance between them.

The shouts of the crowd thundered in her ears.

By lap four Avery heard nothing behind her—no panting, no footfalls. And Thomas was either far enough ahead that she could not hear his shoes hitting the track, or perhaps his gait really was as smooth as it looked. By now he and she were clearly the only runners with any chance of winning.

He seemed to be enjoying a jog in the park.

Avery pushed herself harder than ever. This was so far beyond her training that she realized that had been like child's play. By lap five, just past a quarter mile with that much more yet to go, everything in her screamed to stop. Her every breath burned and her legs felt like lead.

Tears clouded her vision, and she wondered if she would ever see her friends again. Winning looked impossible. Forget an audience with the king. She couldn't even imagine surviving to face the gallows.

By lap six she knew the scouts had to have alerted the council that things looked hopeless for her. She envisioned Tuck pacing—regretting the decision to let her compete— Kate crying, and Kendrick mumbling.

Had the scouts recognized Thomas? Was he the one missing from their number who had *not* been kidnapped but perhaps paid to run *against* the kingdom?

Everyone was right. I shouldn't have run.

What was wrong with Avery that death actually seemed a relief to her now? She began to contemplate the worst way to go.

What if she simply veered off the track and out of the stadium? Could she elude the guards before they realized what she was up to? Sure, her limbs were tying up, her heart and lungs already taxed beyond capacity, and she had no idea if she could reach the cool, dark privacy of the woods.

Could she somehow reach her home, beg someone, anyone, for news of her family, risk everything for one last grasp at freedom?

And if she *were* caught before she escaped the stadium? It would mean the gallows for her anyway, so why not make a desperate lunge for a guard's weapon, take a few of them with her before she was swarmed?

Having completed the seventh lap while entertaining such macabre musings had distracted her, Avery suddenly became aware of every fiber of her being. Not an inch of her body wasn't crying out for rest, for comfort, for oxygen, for water. And yet she also realized she had not lost any more ground to Thomas as they pounded into the first turn on the final 110-yard circuit.

The crowd was on its feet, and it appeared Thomas was finally laboring, too. No human could maintain a sprint for an entire half mile, and he seemed to be working harder to swing his arms, pump his legs. Avery still couldn't imagine catching him, let alone overtaking him, but what did she have to lose if she died trying?

With the roar of the crowd deafening her, she fought to keep her eyes from rolling back in her head. Convinced beyond doubt she was going to die anyway, she kept running as her mind filled with images—images of her dog, her little brother, her mother, her father, all the friends she had made at the castle.

I will *die trying!* she told herself. *I'll spill myself, all of myself, spend all I've got left right here, right now, on this track in front of the king and queen and the scouts and the crowd and everybody.*

She filled the art gallery of her mind with beautiful visions of Kate and Kendrick and Tuck, the dear friends she had come to love.

And Avery realized she had drawn within five yards of Thomas and could actually hear his labored breathing. For the first time he had to have heard or felt or sensed her closing in on him, for he glanced to his right and must have seen her out of the corner of his eye. He wobbled as he appeared to try to accelerate.

Avery lowered her head and tightened her fists and demanded from herself anything more that might be left anywhere deep within her. She willed herself to keep pounding, pounding.

The finish line drew within sight, and Avery's whole body burned. Her bare feet slap, slap, slapped the track as Thomas's shoes kicked grass and soil into her face. And with her last ounce of strength she moved right to pass him.

But he veered to block her!

Avery thrust out her hands to ward him off, then she shot left and dove across the line ahead of him.

Thomas, too, fell and rolled, stopping just short of the finish and having to crawl the last few feet for second place.

Avery lay on her back, gasping, trying to take in that she had actually won. Thomas rested on his side, clasping his chest, shaking violently. She wanted to ask him *why* he had left and *how*, but words were impossible.

Panting, Avery struggled to her feet as men and women rushed to kneel over Thomas. As someone brought her water, she worried he was seriously hurt and wondered whether losing might cost him his life.

⚬✖⚬

A young servant used a gold-handled knife to cut a branch from an olive tree and hand it to an old man leaning weakly on a cane.

"Over here, young man," the old-timer said, extending the branch to Avery, and she realized he was the king! How he had deteriorated even just since she had seen him last!

Though he no longer looked the part of a strong ruler, he certainly appeared pleased by her victory. His alarming green eyes were still bright as sea glass.

This was as close as Avery had ever been to the man powerful enough to, with a single word, spare her life and those of her friends.

Yet she could think of not a single thing to say.

Someone in the crowd hollered, "Say something!"

Queen Angelina, wearing a gold-colored gown with a gaudy gold choker and heavy gold earrings, strode up next to the king. Her fiery red hair cascaded down one shoulder, and Avery thought she would look beautiful if she didn't know how dangerous she was.

The young servant whispered, "Runner, remove your cap in the presence of the king!"

Avery started to curtsy, caught herself, and bowed low.

The servant reached over and angrily yanked off her cap, and Avery's thick mane of dark hair tumbled out.

chapter 13

"Stop Her!"

The crowd gasped, and it seemed all eyes in the stadium had turned to Avery.

"Well, look at that," Angelina said. "A little *girl*!"

"I am not a little girl," she bit back before she could stop herself. "I'm thirteen!"

The crowd rose as the news rippled through the stadium, and Avery could see that the king looked shocked, too. As fast as she could, she bolted from the arena.

"Stop her!" Angelina cried out, but Avery had already recovered her breath and despite aching muscles zipped through the crowd, between the tents, over the hills, back to the castle, and into the Great Hall, glancing over her shoulder before stealing onto the stairwell to safety.

She didn't stop at the bunkroom or even the kids' Great Room.

Avery climbed all the way up and out onto the tiny balcony under the sloping rooftop where she reached to hoist herself up, startled when a hand clamped atop hers.

∞

A strong arm pulled Avery onto the roof.

She landed with a thud, and relief washed over her as she found herself looking into Kendrick's concerned face. He handed her a cloth and a mug of something warm and fragrant, and despite her best efforts, tears began to fall.

"How did you know to meet me here?"

"You underestimate how well I know you."

"You know what just happened?"

He nodded. "It will be the highlight of castle gossip for months."

For once, Kendrick's bluntness comforted her. "What do I do now? I've made a mess of everything *again*."

"Well, you certainly can't risk anyone recognizing you and reporting you to the king. He and Angelina will be turning over every stone to find you as it is."

"No doubt."

"But this will pass, and sooner than you think."

"How can you say that?"

"The king is dying, Avery. Those angling for his throne are moving into the kingdom in droves. A race won by an unknown thirteen-year-old girl will soon be the furthest thing from his mind. He risks dying without an heir—and to a king, little matters more than securing his throne. Having a son or staying alive will soon be all he cares about."

They sat for a long silent moment.

"Thank you," Avery whispered finally.

"I'm just glad you're back," Kendrick said. He pulled from a sack a loaf of crusty bread and a wedge of cheese and handed half to Avery. "You need to get your strength back."

They ate as dusk settled. When a shadow crept across the face of the moon, Avery said, "Shouldn't we go back? Kate and Tuck will worry."

"Wait. There's something you'll want to see."

"I don't think I can handle any more excitement today."

As the minutes passed, the shadow continued to fill the moon until the entire circle of moon was hidden. And then—in a breathtaking instant—the moon reappeared in all its glory, only in brilliant red.

"The ruby moon," Avery whispered. "I've imagined it but never seen it."

"The king planned his Olympiad around astronomers' predictions," Kendrick said. "He calls it 'God's favor.' I call it good timing."

Kate, Tuck, and even Bronte were waiting in the otherwise empty dining room. Despite the time that had passed since the race, Avery felt its effects, plus the fear and the run back to the castle. Her muscles throbbed, and her legs felt like jelly.

If I never run another race, it'll still be too soon.

Kate rushed to Avery and drew her into a hard hug. "What happened?"

As she sat and poured out the story, Tuck draped his coat over her shoulders. Then Kate brought her a bowl of hot broth and more bread. Bronte nudged her cold nose under Avery's hand so she had to pet the dog's silky fur.

Each gesture made Avery feel better.

The group sat contemplating their next move until a scout burst in. "We need to move!" he said. "The king's guard has fanned out searching for the mystery girl who won the race. Castle staff have been put on high alert to find her and report her to His Majesty's people at once!"

Kendrick said, "A few servants know about the kids' quarters. If they breathe a word of it to the wrong person, guards will ransack this side of the castle within minutes."

"Then we need a new place to live," Tuck said. "Now."

chapter 14

The Exodus

"Listen carefully!" Tuck called to the kids assembled in the Great Room. "We don't have much time! We're in danger even as I speak!" They closed in on him in a tight circle.

Avery counted twenty-five and wondered where everyone was then realized that with the disappearances of so many of her peers, this was it.

Tuck continued urgently, "The guards could ransack this side of the castle at any moment, so we need to find new lodging immediately."

One called out, "Is it true that they are looking for Avery?"

Another said, "Where can we go? We have no options."

"The underworld," Tuck said. "Take everything you can carry and move to the tunnels. No time to waste! We won't be coming back to this part of the castle, so don't leave anything you wish to keep."

Kids began grabbing whatever they could carry—

furniture, clothing, books, and blankets—and moving to the stairwell and the library door. Fights broke out over who owned what and who had the right to something that had belonged to someone now missing.

Avery suspected they were arguing over far more than the objects in question.

No one liked the idea of moving on such short notice—and certainly not to the castle's underbelly. In a few hours, this side of the castle would be as empty as the winter woods—and would feel just as cold.

She hurried to the bunkroom to gather her things.

"What an eventful day!" a familiar voice trilled from the doorway.

Everyone stopped, and the room fell silent.

Ilsa glided toward Avery, arms crossed, eyes narrow. "So this is all your fault?"

Avery rolled her eyes.

Ilsa laughed, sounding hollow as the room. "You know more scouts follow you than watch the king? Ironic that you think you're saving us from the evil queen when in reality we're saving you from yourself. And now we move to the tunnels because of you. Where next? The dungeon?"

Avery wanted to protest, but how could she? Ilsa was right.

She was relieved when Tuck appeared, but instead of calling Ilsa out, he whispered, "Why don't you find someplace to wait while we finish here? I'll send someone for you when we're done."

With Bronte at her heels, Avery slipped across the hall into the storage room where Queen Elizabeth's personal things had been kept. The place had been largely picked over for the kids' store, but a few crates remained. She kicked one and bundles of handwritten letters tied with faded ribbons tumbled out.

⁓∞⁓

The kids moved like a great wave of rats into the castle's frigid underworld.

They spent the first night deep in the tunnels—away from the undesirables who occupied the catacombs— bickering and bartering over who slept where and which rooms would be used as common areas. Instead of sleeping in giant bunkrooms as they had upstairs, the kids paired up and claimed smaller spaces. When they found a room they wanted, kids tied a rope between a pair of wall sconces and hung a blanket over it to serve as a door.

With all the blankets, mattresses, and personal

belongings, the tunnels quickly began to resemble the stalls Avery's mother had dragged her to on market days.

Avery and Kate claimed an alcove off the main tunnel away from Ilsa and her friends.

Bronte and her quickly growing litter had free rein of the tunnels and were soon loudly scampering up and down the corridors, barking and nipping and rolling in the sludge.

Avery sensed she would rarely see them in this new home.

❧

Avery—her hair in inky black knots that looked as bad as she felt—went searching for the new dining room and, more specifically, Tuck.

He appeared in a doorway, a kind smile tugging at the corners of his mouth.

"Go ahead," she said, holding out a pair of shears, "laugh. I know I look ridiculous."

"What are these for?"

"Kate won't cut my hair. Someone needs to."

Tuck's face contorted. "Why?"

"It'll give me away. If I look like a boy, maybe they'll

move on. Now come on."

Tuck shook his head, pushing Avery's hand away. "Nobody's gonna find us. I doubt Angelina even knows this place exists. If she does, she's certainly not going to step foot down here."

Avery didn't budge.

"Fine," Tuck said, taking the shears. "Sit."

Avery sat and closed her eyes. She could only imagine what her hair would look like after a thirteen-year-old boy cut it.

This would be such a disappointment to my mother.

She heard the shears open and snap shut a couple of times as Tuck seemed to be practicing with them.

"Ilsa's right, you know," she said. "This is all my fault. I'm sorry we were forced to move here."

"We're here for our own safety," he said. "Forget the race or what you said to the queen. We couldn't stay in the kids' quarters waiting for the next person to disappear. You understand that, right?"

Avery nodded, eyes still closed, fighting tears. "I guess."

The shears opened and Avery tensed.

Then suddenly Tuck said, "I'm not doing this. But I'll tell you what I will do. I'll protect you from anyone who comes looking for you. You have my word."

Avery turned to face him, but he left, taking the shears with him.

She dug in her pocket for a comb and attacked her tangled mess, wondering if Tuck had any idea what he had promised. It was a gallant gesture, and she was touched. She just hoped he wouldn't be put to the test.

She suspected the queen wouldn't give up looking for her so easily.

chapter 15

The Dark-Cloaked Figure

By the next morning, Avery knew the rest of the kids understood two things.

First, they had to be careful. If anyone else living in the tunnels discovered who they were and reported them to the king or queen, that person would become instantly rich and the kids instantly condemned.

Second, deliveries were going to be a lot tougher underground. Matches and candles would have to be smuggled down all the time. And though they'd found space for a large dining table the kids had fashioned out of driftwood, getting food from the kitchens upstairs would require creativity and work. Stragglers in the underbelly would always be threats to steal their next meal, whenever food was delivered.

Breakfast the first morning consisted of meager delicacies the kitchen staff had been able to sneak past the most persistent stragglers. Avery, Kate, Tuck, and Kendrick knew they needed to do something quickly, before mealtimes became too big an ordeal.

The four stayed at the rough-hewn table after breakfast.

"You have it?" Tuck asked Kate, who handed him a velvet pouch. "Nicely done," he said, weighing it in his hand.

"What if no one comes?" Avery said.

"They'll come," Tuck said, confident as a king.

Several more minutes passed, but just as Kendrick let out a sigh, two tall men with unkempt hair, beards like untamed forests, and greasy clothes appeared in the doorway.

Tuck slipped the pouch into his pocket as he stood and extended a hand.

Both ignored it and glared, so Tuck motioned for them to sit.

They looked wary, but they sat, one grunting, "Hear you want peace in these here tunnels."

Tuck nodded. "Don't want any trouble. Just want to get along."

"Who are you?" the other man growled. "Kin tell by your clothes you don't belong down here."

"Secret society," Tuck said. "What do you say we agree to mind our business and you agree to mind yours?"

The men glanced at each other, mumbled something, and nodded. "You were right to come to us," the first said, running stubby fingers through his beard.

"We kin make sure you're left alone," the second said, "but don't 'spect us to do it for nothin'."

"I'm listening," Tuck said, casually putting his hands in his pockets. "What would be a fair price?"

"Scraps," the second man said.

"Excuse me?"

"Offa this here table. We want what's left when you're finished. You gotta get food down here somehow to feed this society o' yers. We ain't askin' fer much."

Tuck squinted and spoke slowly. "You protect our food deliveries, and we give you what's left after each meal?"

"Yessir, that'll do us. Jes' leave it down at the juncture yonder. I kin show ya where I'll be."

"And if I agree to that, you'll shake my hand?"

"Yep."

When they were gone, Tuck said, "And I was prepared to give them enough gold to buy a country house."

❦

During the first week in the underworld, Avery noticed a dark-cloaked figure—head and body bent low—move slowly through the tunnels at the same time each night.

His left foot dragged, and he carried a stick over his shoulder bearing a lantern on one end attached to a hook. Something compelled her to talk to him, but she couldn't imagine what she would say.

Avery vowed to work up the courage to learn more about him.

∞

The twenty-five kids filed into their new makeshift Great Room for midnight court. The space was smaller than it had been upstairs, so they sat shoulder to shoulder, waiting for Tuck to call the meeting to order.

"We have to be quieter here," he began. "You never know who's listening or who they might tell. And we have not simply changed our residence. We have changed our identity. We barely have enough resources to protect and feed ourselves. We're down to scouts and scavengers. Each one of us is now responsible to gather or protect. We must all do our best and not lose heart. We *will* get out of here."

The kids broke into muted applause.

When the meeting ended, Kendrick motioned for Avery to join him, and she followed him into the main tunnel to a tiny alcove where they could be alone, hoping he had news.

He pulled a folded bulletin from his pocket. "Brace yourself," he said.

chapter 16

Hungry Rats

Beneath a headline about the mystery girl who had won the half-mile race, an artist had drawn Avery's face.

"My nose is the wrong size. And my eyes—do they look like that?" Kendrick shook his head. "Good." She handed it back. "Nobody will recognize me from this."

"You don't want to read about the reward for your return?"

"I assume they want me dead, so no, I'd rather not."

"Actually, they want you alive."

Avery took back the bulletin and read the story. The reward was handsome, but indeed, only if she was delivered alive.

Kendrick said quietly, "Only the crown has access to that kind of reward."

"Obviously."

The figure was more than three times her father's annual income. Much as she'd like to believe he was trying to find her and would capitalize on the race to make it happen, she knew otherwise.

"With a reward like that, they must *really* want to find you."

"So let them," Avery said, putting the bulletin in her pocket.

❦

Her afternoons began to consist of sitting beside Tuck in the Great Room listening to the complaints of the kids and the stragglers. Damp, dark days fueled frustrations and allegations, and often the line to speak to him stretched twenty deep.

Tuck would listen, suggest a solution, and send the person or pair on their way.

"He stole my brooch!" one girl accused an old man who lived in the tunnels.

"Do I look like the type of person who would wear a brooch?" the man said.

Avery had to stifle a laugh. She suspected this man was *very* interested in stealing *and selling* brooches.

At night the tunnels belched beggars and thieves onto the streets outside the castle. A beautiful brooch could sell for a pretty penny and the money used to buy whatever an old man desired.

chapter 17

The Night Venture

Distant wailing kept Avery awake long after she should have fallen asleep each night—that, and the bone-chilling dampness that made her toss and turn. She pulled the covers up to her chin to no avail. There weren't enough blankets in the world to make for comfortable sleeping in the tunnels.

But the wailing, oh, the wailing.

Was it a child crying for her mother or a mother crying for her child?

Kate appeared to sleep despite the sound.

But what was that in the darkness on her pillow? Avery strained to see. The ruby ring Kate had received from her grandmother? Whether she had taken it off or it had fallen off, Avery didn't know, but what Kate had told her about it Avery could never forget:

"It belonged to my grandmother. It's a locket. She wrote me this message, but I'll never show anyone what it says."

Avery threw off her blankets and sat up, curiosity intruding like an unwanted visitor.

Kate would never know.

What agony! Avery wanted to read it so badly, yet something compelled her not to move.

Friendship cannot survive if trust is broken.

She slid her legs over the side of her mattress and froze to see if Kate stirred. Her friend looked like the daughter of nobility, her breathing still steady and deep.

Avery battled every impulse and slipped outside their room. Taking a torch from a sconce on the wall, she would find out where the wailing was coming from.

With the torch aloft, Avery navigated the maze that so many came to in order to escape the king's wrath.

As she followed the sound, the louder it grew and the more familiar it sounded.

"Mother?" she whispered, twisting and turning with increased speed.

It was crazy—maybe impossible—but she couldn't imagine happier news than finding her mother in the tunnels. Her mother would know how to fix the mess involving the thirteen-year-olds. And she would do it with her trademark kindness and wisdom. Avery quickly rounded a corner and then another, and suddenly the crying stopped. She stood still and waited, willing it to start again so she could follow the sound.

She considered calling out before realizing her foolishness. Why would her mother have disappeared from their country cottage to hide in the castle's underworld? Angry with herself, Avery turned to go back to bed.

But a hundred feet from where she stood, a cart sat in the center of an alcove.

Had it been there all along? She hadn't seen it a moment ago.

She looked closer and saw that it was not just any cart. The very sight of it made her heart quicken and her eyes fill.

Avery knew from the moment she spotted it that this was the cart that had brought her to the castle. She took a step forward and it rattled, sending her reeling backward.

Another child inside?

She raced to it and yanked back the lid. A pigeon flew out, making Avery shriek. It soared straight up then thudded to the ground. She caught her breath, looked closer, and saw a tiny tube fastened beneath its beak.

"How long were you trapped inside?" she asked, finding a sconce for her torch and picking up the creature so she could open the tube as she had seen her father do a dozen times with his carrier pigeons.

She removed a tiny parchment from the tube and unrolled it.

Avery, agree to help me and I will return you to your family.

Her mind raced with questions, one above all: *How could anyone know I would find the box?*

Whoever brought the bird could still be in the shadows. Avery whirled, senses crackling. Not sensing any movement, she considered what to do next. Not responding was not an option.

Pigeons fly only one direction. Home. I should release this bird back to whoever sent it.

She grabbed her torch and quickly carried the bird to Kendrick's little study near the dining room where he kept a stash of parchment and ink. With the pigeon cradled under her arm, she scratched out:

Tell me more. I will help however I can. Who are you?

Avery blew the ink dry and tucked the message back into the pigeon's tube. She hurried to the base of the stairs that led to the library door.

She hadn't been outside since the race.

Kendrick's warning not to leave rang in her ears, and of course the whole kingdom knew the bulletin offered a huge reward for her capture.

Could someone be trying to draw me out of hiding?

I could be trapped as soon as I step into the library.

But dare I ignore the message?

She climbed the stairs to the library door. It opened with a reluctant groan, and she carefully stepped inside.

chapter 18

Fire!

Moving soundlessly, Avery tiptoed briskly to the kids' stairwell and up to the door that led to the sloping rooftop where she and Kendrick had seen the ruby moon. To her relief, the deserted old quarters lay eerily quiet.

Out on the balcony, she released the bird and it soared into the midnight sky.

As she urgently made her way back, she wondered, *Who knows we moved to the tunnels?*

The next afternoon, the thirteen-year-olds chatted happily over a lunch of boiled meats and thick puddings until two scouts appeared, breathless, wide-eyed, and speaking over each other.

Words rising from the din like *fire*, *king*, *angry*, and *destroyed* sent everyone into an uproar.

With no sign of the rest of the cabinet, Avery stood and

pointed at one of the scouts. "One at a time! You, what's wrong?"

"The Olympiad is in flames!" he said. "The tents, the grounds, everything is on fire. The stadium is destroyed. It's chaos. People are running for their lives, trampling each other on their way to the sea. They say the king is furious, going mad to save his reputation."

As the room dissolved into pandemonium, Avery motioned the scouts to follow her out to where they could talk in peace.

"Are we in danger?"

"If the wind shifts and the flames aren't contained."

"How did it start?"

"Some say it was the king's foolishness—his tent was full of candles."

Avery nodded, remembering her brief time in the king's tent. If even one of those candelabras had been knocked over by an errant elbow, the king's own tent could have gone up in an instant.

The second scout, the mousier of the two, shifted from leg to leg, clearly eager to share his opinion.

"What do *you* think?" she asked him.

"I heard it might have been a plot against the king. He's invited his enemies to compete in the games then put his best athletes up against them. That hasn't won him any friends."

The other scout added, "He *was* in his tent when it erupted. He was lucky to escape."

Avery closed her eyes.

The king believed victory would signal God's favor on his reign.

What would he make of the destruction of the Olympiad by fire?

Avery thanked the scouts and instructed them to return to their posts and keep her updated. She headed back to find Kendrick, Kate, and Tuck. The sooner they assessed what this meant for the kids, the better. One thing was certain: an angry king was a threat to everyone, including himself.

"There is something else," a voice said behind her.

Avery turned to see the mousy scout. "What is it?"

He looked around and approached. "I may know who started the fire." He leaned close and whispered into Avery's ear a name that made her eyes widen.

The rest of the afternoon and evening, reports reached the tunnels of how many had been trampled to death in the stampedes to escape the blaze. Dozens more died trying to put it out.

As quickly as people had arrived from the Salt Sea to watch the great games, they fled. The king's grandiose spectacle had become a colossal tragedy. He was destined to die without an heir and with the Olympiad as his legacy, destroying his reputation.

He retreated to the castle for his own safety, but a castle fraught with distrust was no place to hide.

But did he even know from whom he was hiding?

Knowing one's enemy is half the battle.

chapter 19

The Night Visitor

Avery wanted nothing more than to slip outside and survey the damage. Rumor was, the king's counselors advised he erase all traces of the Olympiad. They even said any unclaimed trampled or charred bodies should be tossed into the Salt Sea by dusk.

Avery was tempted to sneak into the pantry upstairs and spy down into the king's study, but she settled for sitting with the cabinet, waiting for news from the scouts.

"How did you know, Kendrick?" she asked.

"Know what?"

"You predicted from the beginning the Olympiad would end badly."

He looked away and seemed to study the floor. "Just a good guess, I suppose."

"One of the scouts believes the fire was an assassination attempt," Avery said.

Kendrick nodded. "Many would agree."

Avery looked both ways and whispered, "He believes Angelina was behind it."

Kendrick didn't even flinch. "Maybe."

❦

For once Avery slept soundly that night, so it took a moment to realize Bronte's growl was not part of a dream. Her eyes fluttered open to a massive man looming over her.

When she screamed, he quickly limped away, dragging his left leg.

"Stop!" Avery called out as she leapt from her bed. "I command you to stop!" Kate, too, was out of bed in a flash and beside Avery.

A pack of boys appeared out of nowhere, overtaking the man in the main tunnel. They jumped onto his back, but he shook them off like mere grasshoppers.

Spinning around, the man spat, "You're making a scene, which we must avoid! Now, back to bed, children!"

"Not until you tell us who you are," Tuck said.

Kendrick raised a torch, and Avery moved closer for a good look.

It was the figure who moved through the tunnels each night, a stick over his shoulder bearing a lantern. He seemed harmless during the day but looked ferocious at night.

The upper half of his face was pockmarked and scarred, and he wore a thick white beard and a mangy white ponytail. But—despite all that—there was something gentle about the way his mouth curved into a smile.

"Yes," Avery said kindly, moving in. "Who are you?"

Tuck held out a hand to keep her from getting closer.

"Nice of you to protect your girlfriend," the man said, "but despite what you all want to think, I wasn't going to hurt her."

"Then why were you in her chamber in the middle of the night?"

The massive brute looked strong enough to take them all on, but he said, "This is not the time or place, but I'll be back tomorrow morning. We can talk then."

Avery feared if they let him go, she'd never see him again. But what choice did they have? They were no match for him. If he wanted to leave, no one would stop him.

She didn't sleep the rest of the night.

She sat on the floor scratching Bronte's ears and whispering her thanks.

The clatter of cutlery told Avery everyone else was up and eating, but she had no appetite and didn't want to get out of bed.

She desperately wanted a bath to ease her chilled bones, but with no copper basin in the underworld, she would have to settle for lukewarm water in the cleansing alcove. Instead, Avery stayed under her scratchy wool blanket listening to the miserable constant dripping—the first thing she heard every morning and the last thing she heard every night.

Then it hit her. Would the strange man show up as he promised? She scrambled from her bed and dressed, pulling her hair back into a sloppy braid and stepping into her slippers.

Maybe the scouts had discovered something new about him. She swept aside the blanket door—and there he sat, lounging on one of the faded velvet chairs the kids had brought from upstairs, one leg propped on a stool, hands folded on his rotund belly. He had draped his coat over the chair, and his head was tilted back, eyes closed.

Avery cleared her throat.

" 'Bout time you woke up," he said, sitting up. "Been waitin' half the day."

He laughed loudly.

Avery considered calling for backup, but she didn't want him to think she was scared. Plus, he had chosen to come back. How dangerous could he be?

"I'd offer you this chair like a gentleman," he said, "but I've had this limp since childhood that's getting worse with age."

Avery took a stool from her room and sat a safe distance from him. "Why were you watching me sleep last night?"

"Don't enjoy small talk, do you?" he asked with a wink. "Fair enough. I've been sent to keep you safe."

"Yeah, okay, I'll play along. Who sent you to keep me safe?"

"I wish I knew."

"Who are you?"

"Name's Babs."

Avery snorted. "Seriously? Babs? That's a girl's name."

He shrugged.

"Come on. You were sent but you don't know by whom? You didn't show up here on your own. Tell me more."

Babs retrieved from his shirt pocket a large gold coin that

could pay for a month of living in the village. "A fishwife gave me this and asked me to watch out for you. She described you, so I've been searching in each of the chambers. That's what I was doing until your dog got involved."

"Uh, rule number one: watching someone sleep is a bad idea."

Avery had to admit his smile was warm and kind.

"I suppose you're right," he said, "and I apologize for scaring you. The woman will be pleased to know I found you. May I tell her you're safe?"

"Frankly, I don't know how safe I am." Avery wondered if she dared tell this strange man she was at the castle against her will. "First tell me who this fishwife is."

"I don't know."

"What? She pays you that handsome amount and. . .I don't understand."

"She saw me emerge from the underworld and asked me to look for you; that's all I can tell you. I wasn't supposed to say she was even a *she*. But I felt I owed it to you since I frightened you."

"What does she look like?"

"I'd better not say."

"How does she know me? Why does she care?"

"I shouldn't say more. She gave me no reason to think she would harm you."

"At least tell me if she's related to me, knows my family, told you anything more at all—"

The man held up his hands, and Avery knew she would receive no more information.

He labored to his feet with great effort. "I hope at least I've convinced you you have nothing to fear from me. And if you don't mind, I will stay alert to any threats you might face."

"Well, I appreciate that," Avery said, rising to help Babs with his coat. As she moved around behind him to get his arms into it, she noticed peeking from one of his pockets the daily bulletin announcing the reward for her capture. Avery slid it from his coat and slipped it into the pocket of her dress.

Almost taken in by a hearty laugh, a warm smile, and a fishwife tale, she thought, angry with herself. *No wonder he couldn't describe the woman or tell me anything about her. She doesn't exist! Babs, if that's even his name, just wants to cash in on me.*

For the briefest moment, Avery had allowed herself a glimmer of hope.

chapter 20

Queen Kate

Kendrick would know what to do about Babs. She would tell him everything.

But, as usual, he was nowhere to be found.

He had been leaving in the middle of meals and missing council meetings altogether, never offering an excuse.

When Avery couldn't find him in any of the usual places, she instructed a scout to take her to him. The scout hesitated, which only confirmed her suspicion that Kendrick was up to something. "He and I have important business and no time to lose, so let's go."

Clearly reluctant, the scout led her to a tiny room that looked like an ordinary bedchamber and swept aside the blanket partition.

"Kendrick?" Avery called.

He dove in front of an elaborate structure fashioned of tiny wooden planks, his face red as a toddler's caught with his finger in the sugar box.

"Don't blame the scout," Avery said. "I made him bring me."

As the scout retreated, she moved closer to a dazzling miniature replica of the castle—but not *just* the castle— the elaborate stairwell and entire underbelly as well. How much time and energy had Kendrick invested in research alone, not to mention the hours to build this?

"You must have the patience of a saint!" she said, kneeling to peer into the tiny rooms that made up the labyrinth of the castle. "Where did you learn to do this?"

"You're not supposed to be here," he said, wedging himself between her and the model.

"I thought we were no longer keeping secrets from each other."

Kendrick didn't budge. "I never agreed to that. Now *get out.*"

"At least tell me *why* you built this."

Kendrick didn't budge. He stood facing Avery, shielding the replica castle with his body.

Avery stood equally determined.

Kendrick sighed. "I thought it would help us better understand the disappearances. An actual model instead of obscure, hand-drawn maps can maybe tell us where everyone went and lead to better strategies."

Avery marveled at the maze of chambers. "Impressive."

Kendrick's look told her he neither needed nor wanted her approval.

∞

The big news at the next council meeting was Queen Angelina's search for a new lady-in-waiting. Apparently she had dismissed one, accusing her of stealing. That likely meant a death sentence.

"She's looking for intelligence, confidence, and trustworthiness," a scout reported.

"Which rules out anybody I know," Kendrick mumbled.

Avery playfully punched him.

Actually, the idea of planting a thirteen-year-old among Angelina's ladies invigorated the council members, who spent the morning discussing the ways it could benefit them.

"For one thing, first-person access to every decision she makes!" Tuck offered.

"Of course, we also risk one of our own being hung for a false accusation," Kendrick said.

"I say the rewards outweigh the risks," Tuck said. "I'm

open to suggestions for a candidate. The queen interviews applicants in two days at court in the Great Hall."

After the meeting Avery waited for the others to leave before approaching Tuck and blurting, "Consider me."

Tuck smiled, but she couldn't tell if he was amused or willing.

Boys have a peculiar ability to hide their true feelings behind an ordinary smile.

"I'm serious," she said. "I want to be one of Angelina's ladies-in-waiting."

"I know you do," Tuck said finally. "But several have already volunteered, and it's only right and fair that I consider everyone. I can't play favorites, no matter how hard I may want to."

"When will you decide?"

"Tomorrow night."

Late that evening a handful of girls, apparently too excited to sleep, huddled in the sitting room talking about who had the best chance of catching Angelina's eye.

"Think of everything we would get to see and do!" one said.

"How would we know *what* to do?" another asked. "I wouldn't even know how to behave in court during the selection process."

Kate—silent until now—left and soon returned with her wool blanket draped over her shoulders, trailing a drab but impressive train.

"I am Queen Angelina," she announced. "If you would become my next lady-in-waiting, please stand."

Each girl scrambled to her feet.

Kate circled the pack.

"Stand up straighter," she told one.

To another, "Don't look so sour."

"You all need more confidence," she continued. "I cannot abide weak women."

One girl said, "Are we allowed to—"

Kate whirled. "Speak only when spoken to!"

And then to Avery: "Never argue or offer an opinion without being asked."

The playacting went deep into the wee hours, the girls practicing walking, talking, eating, and sitting—all solely to become one long-shot candidate among many in the kingdom for a single position on the court of the most powerful woman in their world.

chapter 21

The Decision

Awaiting midnight court—particularly Tuck's choice of a candidate for Queen Angelina's potential lady-in-waiting—made the next day drag on like a week.

Avery occupied herself with busywork, like helping with breakfast and lunch and assisting Kate with sewing in the afternoon. She sought from the scouts, in vain, anything new about the investigation into the fire, and she spent time exploring more of the underworld.

She still needed to learn whether the tunnels ended at the tiny country chapel on the other side of the Salt Sea. Kendrick wanted to know the same, and Avery was determined to beat him to it. Legend had it that it was nothing like the one in the castle. No, this was a magical place nestled among the cozy, rustic village homes—where the country girls married in unforgettable ceremonies in its unique sanctuary.

Finally the time arrived for the kids to file into their underground Great Room for midnight court. Four chairs had been arranged at the front—one for Tuck and three behind his for Kate, Kendrick, and Avery. A silk flag with the kids' emblem hung on the wall between two sconces, ablaze with the room's only light.

To Avery it seemed a bit much for such a small crowd.

Tuck stood. "We still don't know what's become of our friends," he said, trembling, something he did only when speaking of the missing—which told Avery how heavily they weighed on him. "But I am grateful we have lost no one since moving down here, an idea we can credit to Avery."

He asked her to stand, and she was greeted with enthusiastic applause.

"Let's continue to be cautious, especially when we have to venture back upstairs. Look out for one another and report unusual behavior."

"Okay, enough of that!" a boy hollered. "Can I be lady-in-waiting?" And even Tuck had to chuckle.

"I know that's why we have perfect attendance tonight," Tuck continued, "so about that. . .I had a lot of things to consider, and it wasn't an easy decision."

Kate reached over and squeezed Avery's hand. It seemed the whole room leaned forward.

"I have chosen Ilsa," Tuck said.

Avery sucked in a breath. How was that possible?

Kate whispered, "I don't believe this," but she joined the rest of the girls who clambered to hug and congratulate Ilsa, and Avery knew it would look bad if she didn't. Tuck was talking over the cacophony and she heard him mention her name as well, but little else.

Avery stood on wobbly legs, pasted on a fake smile, and went through the motions of trying to reach Ilsa and pat her on the shoulder. In the frenzy she slipped out of the hall and into the labyrinth to go quietly to her chamber and be alone. Almost as bad as Tuck passing her over was his choosing Ilsa. How could he? Did he not know the real Ilsa?

"Avery," he called from behind her.

She wanted to pretend not to have heard him and just run. But she spun to face him.

"I couldn't choose you after what happened following the race," he said. "What if Angelina were to recognize you in the Great Hall tomorrow?"

"Of course," Avery said flatly, turning away. "How thoughtful of you."

"I had to make the decision I believed was right," he called after her. "One day you'll understand how much you mean to me!"

❧

Avery stalked to her room, yanked the blanket aside, and was about to collapse and sulk in peace at least until Kate returned. But there on her bed sat a crate.

The pigeon has returned!

She pulled open the lid.

Unnerved that the messenger knew where she slept and risked that Kate might find it first, Avery quickly opened the tube to find the message.

Are you prepared to trade everything for your family? Once you leave the underworld, you can never look back.

Of course she was prepared!

But she needed proof her family was safe. She wasn't about to give up the only things she had remaining just to hope she might reunite with her family.

She hurried to where Kendrick kept his model and retrieved parchment and ink from his supplies. *Prove access to my family, and we have a deal,* she wrote.

And as she had the first time, she released the bird from the tiny balcony.

⁂

Later Avery ventured out to find something to distract her. The kids were reenacting Olympiad events in the Great Hall, and she needed to laugh.

"I'm not sure how I feel about this arrangement," Ilsa said, stepping up beside her.

"Oh, please," Avery said. "We both wanted it, and you won. Can't we just leave it at that?"

Ilsa looked confused. "I'm not talking about lady-in-waiting, which I still have to be lucky enough to be chosen for by the queen herself. I'm talking about assigning you as one of my scouts if she *does* choose me."

For once, Avery stood speechless. This was the first she'd heard about that.

Tuck had said nothing to her about becoming a scout.

"What is wrong with you?" Ilsa said. "You were right there when he announced it." Avery shook her head. Ilsa rolled her eyes. "For once, we're on the same team, you assigned to keep me safe, and I'm sure you'd prefer my head rolls. What do I do to make you *not* want me dead?"

Avery enjoyed making Ilsa squirm. She was about to say she wanted nothing, but then she remembered what she wanted. She held out an open palm.

Ilsa scowled. "What?"

"I want my necklace back."

"Your silly red necklace?"

Avery swallowed an unkind reply. Now wasn't the time. "I don't have it."

"You must. You're the one who laughed at it before it went missing."

"For the record, I'm not the *only* one who laughed at it, and I *don't* have it."

Avery dropped her hand and walked away, more certain than ever she would never see that necklace again.

"You still need to tell me what it'll take!" Ilsa called after her, but Avery didn't have the courage to say what she wanted: *Leave Tuck alone.*

chapter 22

The Fishwife

Avery awoke to someone whistling the song she had played for Angelina that had caused the queen to pass out at court. She shuddered to think how close she might have come to being sent to the tower prison over that unintentional choice.

Avery jumped from her bed, threw on her clothes, and followed the sound to the dining area. And there sat Babs.

"Good morning!" he said, mouth full. "You missed breakfast, so I'm eating yours. Hope you're not offended."

He laughed heartily and motioned to a chair across from him, but Avery didn't budge.

"Not offended," she mumbled. "No appetite."

"And I know why," Babs said with a wave. "It was all anyone could talk about at breakfast. Tuck selected Ilsa over you, and you're unhappy about it. C'mon, sit." He shoveled an enormous bite of salt fish into his mouth, making her wonder how he could have been whistling.

"I don't want to talk about it. Anyway, why do you care?"

Babs set down his fork and looked wounded. "And here I thought we were friends."

"What do you want from me?" she asked.

"I want you to sit and keep me company a few moments," he said, his smile returning then fading. "You're angry. What have I done?"

"I don't trust you," she said quietly.

His ice-blue eyes looked genuinely kind, but Avery knew better. She meant nothing but a rich bounty to him. She pulled from her pocket the bulletin she'd pilfered from him and tossed it on the table.

"Found that in your pocket," she said. Babs stopped chewing and folded his meaty hands in his lap. "Friends, are we?" she continued. "You're just here to protect me, look out for me?"

"I can explain," he said weakly.

"Don't bother. I can see what I am to you."

"No, it's not like that. I needed to know who you were. The fishwife described you, but she gave me the bulletin because of the drawing. She told me the eyes and nose weren't quite right, and they aren't, are they?"

Now it was Avery who was taken aback. How could

the fishwife know that unless she was real? "I don't look anything like the drawing," Avery said weakly.

Babs shrugged. "Sure, I knew about the reward. But if I was going to snatch you up, don't you think I'd have done it before now? You've got to believe me. I'm not out to hurt you."

This, at least, made sense. Had she been wrong to assume the worst?

She moved around the table and sat across from him. "Start from the beginning. I have to know who this fishwife is. What can you tell me about her?"

"I've told you all I know! I'd never met her before."

"You said that, but anything, anything at all. A scary presence who intercepted my first visits to the tunnels here smelled like fish. Does she?"

"Well, of course she does!" Babs said, his smile returning. "But all fishwives do! Everybody who works the harbor does. Hey, *I* probably do!"

Avery nodded. "Anything else? Nothing is too insignificant. Her size, shape, an accent, anything?"

Babs pressed his lips together and shoved his plate and utensils aside. "Well, she has strange eyes, I'll say that."

"Strange how?"

"I didn't notice the first time we talked, because it was after sundown and she approached me when I came out of the tunnels. But when I talked to her in the fish market one morning, in fact the morning she gave me the gold coin, the sun caught her full in the face. Those eyes, I'll tell you. . . One is blue and the other brown."

Babs reached for an unused knife and fork, placed them on his plate of half-eaten food, and nudged it across the table to Avery. "You really should eat," he said.

But eating was the last thing on her mind. She rose and solemnly strode back around the table, took the big man's broad face in her palms, and planted a huge kiss on his leathery forehead.

"Why, thank you, ma'am," he said. "I think."

Avery hurried back to her bed where she stretched out and spread open the bulletin. She had looked at it a hundred times since Kendrick first gave her a copy, but now she saw it with new eyes.

Avery had been certain the king and queen were on the hunt for her, but if the fishwife was Queen Elizabeth, and if she had given Babs one valuable gold coin, she, too, might have access to such a handsome reward. It had always niggled at her anyway, why the king or queen wanted her alive when they would probably execute her anyway.

But Queen Elizabeth. *Why would she fake her death? And why would* she *pay to see me alive?*

⁂

Avery stood in the shadows next to Kate as others prepared Ilsa for her big moment.

Ilsa looked strangely beautiful in a high-necked gown of silver brocade. Her smile was too tight, and her eyes lacked the sparkle of sincere happiness, but that dress and the elegant upsweep of her hair gave the illusion of beauty and sophistication necessary to a serious contender for lady-in-waiting.

Most of the ladies in Angelina's court had come to their rank through title or wealth. Ilsa had neither, so the scouts had pickpocketed the wealthy so Ilsa would have enough to appear rich. Her clothes and jewelry completed the illusion, and Kendrick had invented an elaborate past he had drilled into her memory in the short time between Tuck's decision and her appearance at court. Were Ilsa to forget a detail or find herself asked a question they hadn't considered, she was to laugh, flutter her eyelashes, and pretend to be too modest to respond.

The irony.

"I still don't understand why he chose her, Kate," Avery said. "She doesn't know the castle."

"She'll learn. And despite the danger, she *has* agreed to the arrangement."

The arrangement was simple. If Ilsa was chosen, she would gather whatever inside information she could in exchange for the cabinet—Tuck and the council—guaranteeing her protection. Scouts would be stationed strategically to see to that. They established an elaborate code so Ilsa could communicate if she were in danger. Utter the right word and she would be rescued immediately.

Though the role would allow Ilsa to live better than she ever had as an orphan, it came with huge risks.

"She could die," Kate said. "Queen Angelina is petty and impulsive. She accuses her staff of stealing anytime she feels like it. She sent her own cousin to the dungeon when an afternoon tea went poorly."

Creams covered the star on Ilsa's wrist, and she was instructed in no uncertain terms never to roll up the sleeves of her dress for any reason. As they removed the black ribbon knotted at her wrist, her closest friends still hung on her arms and seemed to cling to her words as if this were her last day on earth—which it very well could be.

"Don't be jealous, Avery," Kate said, before she went to stand beside Ilsa. She flipped open a satin-lined box to reveal a necklace of glittering black stones, and Ilsa's friends responded with a chorus of praises.

Kate fastened the necklace around Ilsa's neck and stood back to appraise her. "Stand straight. Be confident. Do nothing risky."

Ilsa actually responded with a laugh, which made Avery turn away.

Ilsa's friends were crying—big, gulping sobs. Ilsa pulled them into a bone-crushing hug, and Avery could tell from the look on her face that she planned never to return. She clearly believed she belonged on the queen's court for real and was destined to remain there for life.

Avery started upstairs to rendezvous with Kate at the same grate from which she had observed the royal wedding. This was one spectacle she couldn't wait to watch unfold.

chapter 23

An Army of Guards

Shoulder to shoulder with Kate, peering down through the grate to where the king and Angelina held court, Avery felt as if the Great Hall itself vibrated with anticipation. Clusters of single girls in glittering gowns and sporting intricate braids appeared to be doing their best to both look demure and draw attention to themselves.

Meanwhile, wealthy dignitaries brought their international scandals and personal squabbles before the king, who arbitrated from his elevated throne. The queen, slouched on her matching crimson velvet perch next to him, seemed to fight to keep her eyes open, twirling a long lock of her red hair around her index finger.

"She's not happy unless she's the center of attention," Kate said. "But she will be soon enough. This has to be the first time a lady-in-waiting will be selected publicly. Ilsa had better get in there. No way she'll be chosen if she's late."

"There she is!" Avery whispered.

Ilsa's graceful entry turned heads, and to Avery's surprise, she actually looked like she belonged. She appeared to introduce herself to some of the other girls and nodded politely to merchants, travelers, and adventurers as she glided into position. Occasionally she raised her chin and laughed, as Kendrick had instructed.

Finally the king concluded his business and ceded the floor to his wife. Oddly, Angelina seemed no more engaged and, still slouched and twirling her hair, whispered instructions to an aide. He barked at the candidates to line up, and as he called their names they advanced before her throne one at a time, curtsied, and nervously answered her questions.

One girl didn't hear her name at first, and when the aide had to repeat it, the queen bellowed, "Never mind! Dismissed! Next!"

Another advanced too quickly and had to catch herself to keep from stumbling. She said, "Forgive me, Highness."

Queen Angelina peered down upon her as if she were a smudge on one of the stained-glass windows. "I beg your pardon, young lady! Did someone ask you a question?"

"No, Your Ladyship. I just—"

"You spoke without being spoken to in the royal court, my dear. Next!"

When the young woman burst into tears, the festivities had apparently, finally, captured the queen's attention. She sat up and raised a hand. "Ladies, your responsibilities will largely consist of representing the throne during functions much like this one. How you comport yourself here reveals your abilities—and limitations. It should come as no surprise that I seek someone with the ability to pay attention, respond with dispatch but not carelessness, decorum, and certainly no displays of emotion. Carry on."

The queen asked several of the girls their family histories, their educational backgrounds, their interests and talents, and why they wanted to serve in her court. She dismissed some, midsentence, as too loud, two as too soft-spoken, one as too tall, and three as too fat.

To another she was particularly cruel.

The girl had curtsied and stood waiting as Queen Angelina merely stared down at her. Finally, as if surprised she was still there, she said, "Turn right. Now left. Now face me again." Still the queen looked only curious, cocking her head as the girl flushed. "Repeat your name." When she did, Angelina said, "Do you have family at court today?"

"My parents are, Your Highness, yes."

The queen instructed her aide to call on them to identify

themselves. From near the back of the hall, a tradesman and his wife in drab clothing stood, the man quickly removing his cap and smoothing his hair. He attempted an awkward, sweeping bow, and the woman a self-conscious curtsy as the queen stood as if to get a better look.

"I should have known," she said, slumping back to the throne. "That answers any questions about pedigree, young lady. As for you folks, enjoy your day at court! First time here?" The man grinned and waved, and his wife grabbed his arm. "Well, you should have saved whatever you spent on this dress. If I were choosing dresses, she might have a chance, but she's got a face for the farm. Next!"

A murmur swept through the Great Hall.

"Do you believe that?" Kate said. "Who would want to serve such a horrid witch?"

"Ilsa will fit right in."

"Avery!"

The girl's father appeared to shudder with rage as his wife wrapped him in her arms and pleaded with him to sit.

Though the girl herself had been dismissed, she appeared to be going nowhere. "Speak to me any way you wish, Highness," she said, "but I will not have you humiliate people I—"

"Careful, miss!" the queen's aide said, and like a flash a young man raced from behind a pillar and escorted the girl out.

"Yes!" the queen snapped. "Watch your tongue! I've had vixens executed for less."

"Kate!" Avery said. "Wasn't he one of ours?"

"He was! That was our mousy scout, assigned to Ilsa! What got into him? He'd better hurry back."

The next half dozen candidates approached the queen warily, and most she dismissed with a wave in the middle of their answers to innocuous questions.

Finally, with eleven more candidates to go, the aide called for Ilsa. With all that had transpired, Avery thought she might actually have a chance to impress. And though Avery was disappointed not to be the candidate herself, she couldn't deny the advantage it would be to the kids if Ilsa won. She found herself pulling for her rival in spite of everything.

Ilsa appeared not to have been rattled by the earlier confrontation and did well remembering her invented history. She may have gone a bit long with one of her answers, and it appeared the queen might be losing interest. But Ilsa signaled the mousy scout, who dramatically reappeared, facing the queen with an elaborate wooden box. At Ilsa's request he raised the lid, and Angelina rose from her throne.

"For me?" she said.

Ilsa curtsied anew. "Your Highness."

"What's in the box?" Avery whispered.

"The result of much pickpocketing," Kate said.

Angelina descended the throne and lifted one of the coins to the sun before returning it to the box. Scanning the ten remaining candidates, she said, "Did any of the rest of you think to bring your potentate a gift? Or did you assume today was all about you?"

She turned back to Ilsa. "Well played, dear."

And then to the scout: "As for you, knave, what was your connection to the other girl, the homely, impudent one?"

"None, Majesty."

"Yet your swift action spared her life. Why?"

"It seemed her motive was loyalty, Highness, not disrespect."

The queen turned back. "Ilsa, is it? This is your servant? Keep him close." She sauntered back up the steps to her throne and sat then beckoned Ilsa to follow.

Ilsa self-assuredly gathered her skirt and climbed to stand before the queen, who spoke so softly it was clear no one else heard. Ilsa bent and whispered in Angelina's ear. The queen arched a brow and, for the first time, smiled.

Angelina instructed Ilsa to stand next to her with her hand on the armrest of the throne. "Now, allow me to repeat my question to the ten remaining candidates," she said. "Did any of you think to bring a gift to your queen? Anyone? No one?

"Knave, again, I commend you for your valor. Leave the tribute with my aide as you depart. And now, Your Royal Highness, members of the court, honored guests, and beloved subjects: it gives me great pleasure to introduce the newest member of my court, a lady-in-waiting, Ilsa!"

⟨∞⟩

That night, in her new role as one of Ilsa's scouts, Avery knelt at her assigned grate and peered into the queen's private chamber. Ilsa and her new lady friends giggled over some whispered gossip until Angelina burst in and the laughter ceased.

The queen marched to the center of the room and paced. "If I can't give the king an heir, he'll kill me just as he did Queen Elizabeth. If I don't stop him, he'll put a stop to me."

Avery couldn't believe it!

Queen Elizabeth wasn't killed. She died hours after giving birth. Or did she?

Angelina approached Ilsa and clutched her wrist so tightly that Ilsa's face drained of color. "I must take matters into my own hands. Will you help me?"

Angelina was close to exposing the star on Ilsa's wrist. Avery wondered if she should alert the other scouts, but she couldn't pull away.

Ilsa said, "Whatever you ask."

"Good," Angelina said. "It may have to happen tonight."

With these words, Avery ran for the tunnels.

∞

Hours later, Avery sat with Kate and smiled at Babs across the Great Room as he watched a bunch of boys enjoy a noisy game of pins. They had whittled the pins out of wood and now tried to knock them down with a ball. Babs had joined them for the afternoon, and Avery got a kick out of the way he stood out like a sore thumb. He had become a regular fixture at meals and during their activities, the gentle giant with a funny line or wise suggestion.

"I brought you something from the fishwife!" he called to her.

Avery was curious but didn't want to interrupt a perfect evening. She had wheedled a few sheets of parchment out of Kendrick and drawn caricatures of her friends while Bronte lay at her feet, raising her head only when someone laughed or shouted. Avery laid her hand atop the dog's silky head, and her eyes brightened at the attention.

A scout raced in—winded and wide-eyed. "They're coming!" he said, gasping.

That got Tuck's attention. "Who?"

"Guards. Lots. Of. Guards. Either you guys were too loud or someone must have told them we were here."

Avery shot Kate a knowing glance. *Ilsa!*

Was that how she had made the queen smile? Had she promised Angelina some inside information and had now delivered?

The rumble of approaching footsteps became overpowering.

"Hide!" Babs growled. "All of you, out of here, now!"

The thirteen-year-olds scattered like cockroaches, darting in every direction, upending game boards and leaving balls and books. Some took off down the main tunnel, others into the shadows or around corners out of sight.

Avery bolted into an alcove away from the light of

torches, Kate close behind.

"Do not move," she whispered. "No matter what. Promise?"

But even she had no idea how long they could elude an army of royal guards.

chapter 24

The Devastating Death

Avery peered around the corner at guards wearing breast-plates, hoisting torches, and brandishing swords.

"Out of our way!" one hollered.

Babs had planted himself squarely in their path. "What's going on?" he said calmly. "My friends and I live here in peace. How can we help you?"

"The queen's diamond coronation necklace is missing," the guard grunted.

Avery shook her head. *They're not looking for the necklace. They're looking for us!*

Kate drew a finger to her lips.

"I've nothing to hide," Babs said, "but leave my friends alone. They have nothing that belongs to Her Majesty."

The guards mumbled, their crashing and bashing echoing off the walls, reminding Avery of the night that squatters destroyed her mother's best dishes. She winced at each new clash and clatter, wondering if any of their belongings could survive.

"I didn't take it!" Babs cried out. "Unhand me! I had nothing to do with it. I've never seen that necklace before in my life!"

"Oh no," Kate whispered. "You think they found it on him?"

"Wherever they say they found it, they had to have planted it," Avery said. "I trust him, and none of us would have taken it."

"And what's this?" a guard bellowed.

"That's mine! I didn't steal that!"

"That's a heavy piece of gold for a man like you."

"I earned that!"

"We'll see about that. It's the kind of coin bestowed by kings or queens. How'd you come by it?"

"I told you, I earned it! Take your hands off of me! I'm innocent!"

"Tell that to the throne! To the dungeon with him!"

Avery could barely keep herself from rushing to his defense—but Kate must have sensed it. She grabbed Avery's wrist.

It was a good thing, because it was clear Babs tried to fight for his freedom. And not even a man of his size and strength was a match for armed guards.

Grunts, clangs, a cry of pain. Avery prayed Babs would just surrender so they wouldn't run him through with a sword.

A sickening crack was followed by a whine. *That didn't sound like Babs!* In fact, it hadn't sounded human.

Then Babs said weakly, "I didn't do it! Let me go!" as he was plainly being dragged away.

As if he had gathered a last ounce of strength, Babs's shout reverberated off the walls: "Find me! Don't forget me!"

And Avery knew it had been directed right at her.

∝∞‿

Everything became unnaturally quiet.

When Avery finally peered around the corner, cold dread shot through her.

Bronte lay motionless where the guards had been.

"No!" she said, gasping, but as she stepped out, Kate yanked her back into hiding.

"Wait! Someone could still be watching."

"I don't care!" She wrenched free and ran to kneel beside her dog. "Bronte," she cried, running her hand over the furry head and trying to rouse her.

A gaping wound in Bronte's side revealed where

someone had thrust a knife.

Hot tears coursed down Avery's cheeks and splashed onto Bronte's fur. This dog had been her best friend for as long as she could remember. They had grown up together, running through the woods. Henry held Bronte's tail when he was learning to walk. Bronte had been a constant, comforting presence in their lives before and after Avery and Henry lost their mother. Avery and Bronte had spent countless nights in her castle tree house while she dreamed of better days.

Time seemed to stop as she grieved, memories rolling through her mind. Though it felt like hours, mere minutes passed before Kate, Kendrick, and Tuck joined her and dropped to their knees, petting Bronte and whispering condolences.

"Why Bronte?" Avery said as she rocked on her knees. "She had nothing to do with the queen's necklace."

"And neither did Babs," Kendrick said. "But you know Bronte had to be trying to defend him or she wouldn't have been attacked."

That thought made Avery proud but also cut through her and shot guilt to her heart. Babs could be in the Tower by now, or worse, he could be dead by supper—hung before a crowd of cheering villagers. Angelina was known to send thieves straight to the gallows.

"All this because the queen is so selfish," Kate said.

She, Tuck, and Kendrick helped Avery to her feet as a group of scouts arrived and asked if they could take the dog. "What will you do with her?" Avery managed, knowing they didn't have much choice. She would wind up at the bottom of the Salt Sea. "You'll wrap her with dignity, won't you?"

"Of course," a scout said.

"And don't let her pups see her."

"If we can help it."

"Can I have one more minute?" she said.

"Hurry," the scout said.

In tears, she knelt again and laid her head on Bronte's matted fur the way she had as a child. As she gathered the warm, lifeless body into her arms, Avery felt something sharp and jagged beneath the dog. She surreptitiously closed her hand around it and stood to make way for the scouts.

As they gently lifted Bronte onto a blanket to carry her away, Avery told her friends she wanted to be alone for a while. Kate said, "We're going to look for the pups."

"I appreciate it."

When they were gone, she hurried to her room and opened her hand, praying she wouldn't find Queen Angelina's diamond coronation necklace.

She didn't.

It was the ruby flower necklace. Could this be what Babs said he had brought her from the fishwife?

chapter 25

Secret Meeting

As if the kids hadn't lost enough already, the guards had ransacked their rooms, upending beds, rummaging through trunks, ripping clothes, trampling linens, and breaking furniture.

They worked silently and somberly late into the evening putting everything back in order, and they would need to rebuild their lives again, too.

Fortunately, and remarkably, the scouts reported that the royal guards told Queen Angelina they had found no colony of thirteen-year-olds in the tunnels. But the scouts also said they had not seen Ilsa since the incident either. Naturally, no one knew whether she had left on her own, been dismissed, or was in mortal danger.

❦

Avery sat alone on her bare mattress, not motivated to put her room back together. Several of her books had been ripped, her jeweled dagger was missing, and her gowns lay trampled in a heap, but she didn't care. Bronte was all that mattered.

Avery wrapped her fingers around the ruby flower necklace, grateful to have it back. She quickly concealed it when her blanket door swept aside and Tuck appeared.

"You could have announced yourself," she said.

"Right, sorry," he said. "Won't happen again. Listen, if Ilsa gave us away, we have to find her and silence her."

"We don't even know where she is or if she had anything to do with this," Avery said, narrowing her eyes.

"We both know she had everything to do with this," Tuck said. "She knows too much."

"If she gave us away, it's a little late to silence her, wouldn't you say?"

"What if she tells someone where we're hiding?" Tuck said. "We don't have enough scouts to stand sentinel all night watching for an ambush."

"*Another* ambush, you mean?" Avery said. "What do you call what just happened?"

"They didn't know who they were ransacking. They thought we were Babs's people." Tuck's eyes widened.

"What if Ilsa tries to collect a bounty for exposing us?"

"Who would she tell, and who would believe her? She would be implicating herself. She'd better pray nobody finds the star on her wrist."

"I wish I shared your confidence," Tuck said, shaking his head as he was leaving. "But I have to admit you were right. I never should have put Ilsa up for lady-in-waiting."

⸎

Alone again, Avery examined the necklace for signs that it might open. Though it was heavy, she had not considered it might be a locket until Kate had showed her her grandmother's locket ring.

The ring and the necklace looked as if they could have come from the same collection. Discovering a tiny hinge on one side, she pressed it with her thumb.

And just like that, it opened.

To Avery's disappointment, she found no tiny message inside, but she did find something else. On one half was a tiny sketch of Queen Elizabeth—no surprise. Avery had long suspected she originally owned the necklace.

But the tiny rendering on the other side caught her off

guard. An infant, but familiar.

"Kendrick," she whispered, smiling.

But why would my mother give me a locket containing a portrait of Kendrick, let alone the queen? And how did it end up under Bronte's body?

Babs must have had it.

At the sound of a rustle, Avery quickly slipped the necklace into her pocket.

A girl she didn't recognize swept aside her blanket door. She had raven hair and troubled blue eyes. "I need your help," she said. "Follow me."

⚬⚭⚬

The longer they walked through the web of alleys and tunnels, the more Avery wished she had refused or asked a lot of questions before following the girl. In her grief, she hadn't thought clearly about the danger in following this girl. She had simply welcomed the distraction.

For all Avery knew, she was about to come face-to-face with Ilsa.

The girl stopped and motioned for Avery to go on without her.

A few tentative steps led to a large, airy chamber

shrouded in shadows where a young man stood with his back to her.

"Hello?" she called tentatively.

He turned. She gasped.

chapter 26

Evidence!

"I hoped for a moment alone with you again," the young man said, with what appeared to be a phony smile. It was the long-lost Edward, and he was shivering. "I suspect the cold and damp are constant down here?"

Avery nodded, kicking at the tunnel floor with her slipper. She had been certain when she bade him good-bye after he brought her back to the castle that she would never see Edward again. And if she were honest, that would have been fine with her. "How did you know where to find me?"

He laughed. "I'll take that as a welcome."

But when he stepped toward her, Avery stepped back. "Answer me. Who told you I was here?"

"Does it matter?"

"It does if I'm going to trust you."

Edward's smile vanished. "We were friends. What's happened?"

"Everything's happened. Earlier today your sister disappeared."

Avery waited for this news to alarm him, but it didn't.

"Why are you here?" she pressed.

And then it hit her. *The carrier pigeons! He sent them. Of course! They belonged to my father, and Edward is still squatting in my family home.* Why had it taken her so long to figure that out?

Edward began to answer, but Avery put up a hand. "Can you prove my family is alive?"

He smiled. "Smart girl. I thought you might ask." He reached into his shirt pocket and extended a fist to her. He slowly opened his fingers.

Henry's paper boat!

She reached for it and gently turned it over to survey the smudges where Henry's pudgy fingers had folded and refolded it, so important had it been to him to get every detail right. Their last day in the woods, he had tucked it in his pocket to take to a nearby stream. He chattered nonstop about it as they walked.

"Do you think it will float?"

"What makes boats float?"

"You should make one so we can race!"

She had been annoyed by his jabbering, sulking that she had to spend her birthday taking care of him. Now she swallowed a tide of emotion. They'd never made it to the stream, and she would give a hundred birthdays just to spend one afternoon racing paper boats with Henry, questions and all.

"Where is he?" she asked.

Edward cocked his head. "You know the rules. You agree to help me, and I return you to your family. I need to know you'll uphold your end of the bargain."

"How do I know this isn't a trick?" she asked.

"You don't, but what do you have to lose?"

"Why do you need my help?" she asked. "You were a scout, and you know I botch every attempt to be helpful."

Edward smiled. "Best to have on one's side those with the most to lose if you fail. You, dear girl, are fighting for your family. What could be more important than that?"

Avery desperately searched Edward's face. "Please tell them I love them and that I'm coming for them as soon as I can."

"Tell them yourself," he said with his trademark confidence. "Meet me in the chapel on the other side of the Salt Sea in five days, and I promise to reunite you with your family before month's end."

Avery turned the paper boat over and over and sighed.

"I've heard so much about that wonderful place, I actually began to wonder if it really existed. How do I get there?"

But when she looked up, Edward had gone, his footsteps fading.

⸎

The next morning Avery met with Kate, Kendrick, and Tuck and said, "We need to find where they're holding Babs."

The others looked at each other before Kendrick finally spoke. "Avery, you need to face the reality that they've probably already executed him."

"But if not? He told us to find him!" she said. "We have to at least try. What if he's still alive and counting on us?"

Kate nodded. "She's right."

"Fine," Kendrick said. "But don't get your hopes up. I'll see what the scouts can do to help, but getting into the Tower will be dangerous."

"We owe it to him," Avery said. "And there's something else. I don't believe the king is dying of natural causes. He's being poisoned, and I need you to help me prove it."

"No one is poisoning the king," Kate said with a wave. "You know how difficult it would be to slip anything into his food or drink? Everything is first tested by a taster."

Avery nodded. "Which is why whoever's poisoning him has to be someone he trusts—like Angelina. Look at his symptoms. It's not impossible."

Kate shook her head. "If Angelina doesn't have a son with the king, it would not be in her best interest to kill him."

"Which is why I suspect she already has a baby on the way."

"Still too much risk," Kendrick said. "What if her baby's a girl?"

Tuck nodded. "Right. The only way she could risk poisoning the king was if she knew he had an heir to the throne. And since we all know he doesn't, we can be sure the queen wouldn't kill him."

Avery held Kendrick's gaze. *It's time to tell your friends that the king's blood flows in your veins.*

chapter 27

Kate's Secret

Avery, Kate, Tuck, and Kendrick gathered in a tight circle in a room in the kids' old quarters upstairs and looked down through the grate to where the king lay surrounded by a handful of his closest advisers.

He looked gravely ill.

If the scouts' reports were accurate, he was about to undergo a procedure that could cost him his life.

Angelina paced nearby, her ladies-in-waiting lurking in the doorway.

Avery sucked in a breath as the medic wielded a glinting knife and the advisers made room. "Brace yourself, Your Majesty."

He drew the blade across the king's skin, and the king moaned and closed his eyes. For an instant Avery thought he might be dead already. A line of deep red crossed his arm and pooled into a tiny bowl.

"Barbaric!" Avery whispered.

"No!" Kate said. "Everyone knows bleeding is best."

Ten minutes later the medic dressed the wound and said, "Now we wait and pray while he rests and nature takes its course."

Avery knew he meant, *Either way, don't blame me.*

∞

When the four council members disbanded, Kate went her own way without a word, leaving Avery with a sudden urge to follow her.

She gave Kate a head start and then took a new route that led to a room above the king's private dining area. But regardless what grate she peered down through, Avery saw no sign of Kate. Finally she heard her friend's familiar laugh and looked down into a small kitchen beside the dining hall where the king and queen were usually served.

The staff seemed to be in a frenzy as someone called out items to prepare for the king in case he awoke hungry. With still no sign of Kate, Avery was about to move on when she heard her familiar voice.

Kate, unhappy, appeared. "You must work faster!" she said, inches from a cook's face. "His Majesty could awake at any moment. We can't tell him we have nothing, can we?"

The plainly frightened cook shook her head.

But as she got a better look, Avery realized the young woman only looked like Kate, but she was older! Could it be that Kate was not an only child? This girl must have been the one who accompanied Angelina upstairs the night before the wedding to see her gown. It hadn't been Kate after all!

But why wouldn't Kate have ever mentioned a sister?

And if she has an older sister working in the castle, why is Kate hiding among us thirteen-year-olds?

The young woman with Kate's voice ordered everyone else—including the cook—to carry out platters immediately for the queen and her court. Avery was about to go look for Kate when Angelina suddenly arrived.

A queen had no reason to enter a kitchen, especially when her husband was on his deathbed. Angelina looked over her shoulder, eyes darting.

"Did you bring it?" she asked.

The woman who looked and sounded like Kate slipped a hand into her pocket and handed a tiny box to Angelina, who dumped its contents into a goblet and quickly stirred.

"You know what to do with it," the queen said, handing her the goblet and patting her on the shoulder before sauntering out of the kitchen.

Avery could hardly believe it! If Angelina *was* poisoning the king, just as she suspected, Avery had to act quickly.

Is it possible Kate knows?

Avery would be racing the clock, so she would start by telling Kendrick. He'd know what to do about Kate.

chapter 28

The Locket

Avery met Kendrick on the rooftop that overlooked the sea and blurted what she had seen.

He lay back, propping himself on his elbows and staring at the stars, hardly the response she expected. "And you're sure this *powder* was poison?" he asked, his voice as dismissive as she had ever heard it.

"Of course! She told the girl she knew what to do with it. What else would it be?"

Kendrick shook his head and met her gaze. "Avery, you're overreacting. The king is on his deathbed, likely being fed every imaginable herb and potion to help him rest and heal, and you jump to the conclusion that some powder his own wife adds to his drink is poison?"

"I know what I saw, Kendrick. I watched the queen clear the room before adding the powder—"

"Come on, Avery, you can't even keep your story straight. You said the girl who looked like an older Kate sent everyone out first and that the queen looked around to make sure no one else saw her in there."

"Okay, so I'm upset. Regardless, why would Angelina have to do it herself, and why secretly?"

Kendrick shrugged. "Why does she do anything she does?"

"Well, did *you* know Kate's older sister worked in the castle?"

"No, and neither do you! You're just jumping to another conclusion! Just because this girl looks like her and sounds like her doesn't make it so. Kate's never mentioned anything about a sister."

"I know, but that doesn't mean it's not true either."

They sat watching the waves crash against rock.

"But think about it, Avery. Why would Kate hide a sister from us?"

She shook her head. "I don't know, but I think we need to find out. None of this makes sense to me. Don't you wonder what happened? How did you get sent away and mistaken for dead? And why? The king had every reason to be the happiest man on earth."

Kendrick shrugged. "My mother died within hours of my birth. He was probably so overcome with grief about her that he believed whatever they told him about me and never gave me another thought."

"I'm sure that isn't true. Someone else wanted you dead, and I think the king thinks you are. You know Queen Elizabeth didn't want you harmed."

Kendrick laughed. "It must be nice to believe whatever you want to just to make you feel better."

"I *do* believe the queen is still alive."

Kendrick sat up and looked deep into her eyes. "My mother? What are you talking about?"

Avery told him about the fishwife and how Babs had described her eyes.

He sighed heavily. "Does that fanciful mind of yours ever stop? We have really got to find you more to occupy your time."

Avery pulled the ruby necklace from her pocket, popped open the locket, and showed Kendrick the image of the baby. He studied it a long time, tipping it to get the full light of the moon on it. "It's not me, Avery. Look. The nose is wrong."

Avery took the locket back and shifted so she could hold it near Kendrick's face. She had been so sure. But he was right. "Then who could this be?"

"Avery," Kendrick said solemnly, "look very closely. Do you know who I see?"

"Who?"

"It looks like *you*."

Avery laughed and smacked him on the shoulder. "You're funny! Why would my face be in a locket alongside an image of the queen?"

Kendrick shrugged. "Your mother loved the queen. Makes sense that she would put your faces side by side in a special piece of jewelry."

"Nah, I don't know."

As they crawled down, Kendrick said, "A mother's love always outlives her."

❧

Because of the damp conditions of the underworld, thirteen-year-olds began getting sick, starting with a cough that became something more sinister deep in their chests.

One morning, after three kids were found sick in their beds, Kate called an emergency meeting of the cabinet. She showed up with a stack of clean blankets. "We need to move everyone who is sick until they are well again."

"A makeshift infirmary," Avery said.

Kate nodded. "We'll forbid visits, and I'll look after them."

"Tuck and I can do the heavy lifting," Kendrick said. "We'll find and secure the right location and start moving them."

Avery wished more than ever that Babs was still around. He would know what to do. Plus, he could carry the beds over his shoulder in half the time it would take the thirteen-year-olds to do it like ants on a hill. It struck Avery that the kids could die in the underworld without the right kind of help.

Kate asked Avery to cut the blankets into strips. "We need to make cloths from them we can soak in warm water and use on the patients."

⸎

As the council broke up, Avery grabbed Kendrick and motioned for him to follow her to a private spot. "You can't go anywhere near the infirmary," she whispered, "once even one patient is moved there."

"Why?"

"Do I need to remind you that you could be the next king?"

Kendrick drew a finger to his lips. "So what am I supposed to do, stand around and watch? You don't think the others will notice I'm not helping?"

Avery pointed to the blankets. "Start tearing these into strips."

Something scuttled in the shadows, making Avery hope she hadn't been overheard.

chapter 29

Secrets

Avery peeked into their chamber as Kate sat on the corner of her own bed, pinning her hair.

Kate was meticulous about the way she got ready each morning, and today was no exception. First she washed her face. Then she dressed, fixed her hair, and then—when she thought no one was watching—carefully reapplied the star to her wrist using paint from a tiny porcelain jar she kept hidden.

"Why didn't you tell me about her?" Avery asked.

Kate jumped, whirling so quickly she knocked the porcelain jar from the mattress, spilling ink onto the floor.

Both girls stared at the jar, neither moving to clean the mess.

"Tell you about whom?" Kate asked, straightening.

Avery came to sit beside her on the bed, carefully stepping over the spill. "I know about your sister. I saw her in the kitchen."

Kate shook her head, furrowing her brow. Was it possible Kate didn't *know* she had a sister? The castle was full of secrets, after all. But then her lower lip began to quiver, and all Avery's questions came flooding back.

"You can tell me, Kate. Really, you can."

Kate crossed her arms, making Avery assume she was going to deny it. But she said, "Her name is Edith, and she and I have had little to do with each other since childhood. There are things you don't know about me, and it's better this way."

Avery shook her head. "Don't you think it's time we tell each other everything? Why do you need to keep Edith a secret? Maybe she could help you—help *all* of us."

Tears clouded Kate's eyes. "Someday you'll understand. For now you need to trust me."

But Avery was tired of secrets. "Let's start with this," she said. She took Kate's arm and turned her hand over. "Why don't you have a permanent star like the rest of us?"

Kate lowered her head, and it was as if she had to squeak out the words. "Because I'm not thirteen."

Who in the world was this, and how old was she? Avery sensed she was on fragile ground. "You once told me it was your job to keep me safe. What did you mean?"

Kate shrugged, pulling away and crossing her arms. "My grandmother told me she was bringing you to the castle and that it was my job to look after you. She said you were hard to tame and worried you would try to run away. I promised to help. After she died, I considered sneaking out, but where would I go? And anyway, you're the first real friend I've ever had."

Avery let that sink in.

"Aren't you going to ask how old I am?"

"I assume you'll tell me when you're ready."

"Fifteen."

Because she was Kate's friend, Avery vowed to herself she would never reveal Kate's secrets to anyone in the world, no matter the consequences.

chapter 30

Dead

Avery joined a group of kids in a midmorning round of bandy ball, using bats to hit a ball through rings wedged into the tunnel floor.

She was practicing her swing when a scout approached, one she recognized who'd spent a lot of time talking strategy with Tuck. "Want to join us?" she asked, but he shook his head, leaned close, and whispered in her ear.

Avery dropped the bat and ran down the tunnel.

One of the players called after her, but she refused to stop until she reached the tiny alcove where Tuck had lodged his mattress. She swept aside the curtain only to find the alcove empty. So it was true?

"No!" she said, running farther, checking chambers as she ran. "Please!" she prayed.

She arrived at the infirmary out of breath, frantically peering into each tiny chamber until she came to Kendrick and Kate standing over a patient. They turned to her, their expressions heavy.

Avery pushed between them to where Tuck lay motionless, face pale and forehead damp. She willed his chest to rise and fall but detected no movement. Horrified, Avery considered everything she and he had left unsaid. She needed his friendship as fiercely as the rest of the kids needed his leadership.

"When he didn't show up for breakfast," Kendrick said, "I found him like this."

Tuck's eyes fluttered open and closed again.

"Tell me he'll be all right," Avery said.

Kendrick and Kate glanced at each other, and she finally muttered, "I'm afraid he needs remedies we don't have."

Avery's mind raced. Surely the castle had medics with a tonic that could heal a thirteen-year-old boy. And then it hit her. "Kendrick! You need to get out of here!"

He left immediately, and strangely, Kate didn't ask any questions.

❦

Hours later, Avery remained sitting alone beside Tuck's sickbed. Against her better judgment, she touched his forehead and felt the fever then took his cold hand in both of hers.

She asked God to spare his life and whispered words she'd heard her mother pray, "You give and You take away. Blessed be the name of the Lord."

Even as she prayed, she knew she needed to take her mother's advice and go to the chapel.

There were things she wanted to say to Tuck, but her thoughts were jumbled, and she remembered only their needless arguments, the unheeded advice, and the wasted time.

For hours she did not leave his side. She sent a scout for one of her books then alternated reading and praying. She prayed that God would spare Tuck's life. And she prayed that God would keep Babs safe—wherever he was.

Kate checked on Tuck every half hour or so, but she couldn't confirm he would survive. Only when she insisted Avery go to supper did she leave, wondering if she would ever see Tuck again.

Returning to her bedchamber after supper, Avery had to smile.

The familiar wooden crate lay on her bed.

In truth, she was relieved. She had already decided to

send Edward a message telling him she needed more time. She didn't dare leave Tuck sick in his bed, and she was sure Edward would wait.

She opened the lid and jumped back. Steadying herself, she peeked into the box again.

The bird lay motionless, its neck at an odd angle.

How long has the poor thing been in here?

She knew better than to touch a dead, potentially diseased fowl, but she needed to see what message it carried. She eased her hand in, trying to reach the tube without touching the bird.

Suddenly, she heard Kate's voice and looked for a place to hide the crate. The box was too large, and she knew her only option was to distract Kate. Pressing the box against the wall, she perched on a corner of the mattress right as Kate swung the blanket aside.

"Just came to check on you," Kate said. "What's that behind you?" Avery shrugged. Kate peered over her shoulder. "What's in the box?"

"Nothing that concerns you," Avery said, but Kate reached behind her and pulled it out. "Please don't open it."

But of course Kate did, and she shrieked as the bird fell to the floor. "Why do you have a dead bird in our room?"

"You have your secrets, and I have mine!" Avery said, knowing this might be her only chance to check the bird's tube for a message. But as she scrambled to get to it, she wondered what she would say if the message revealed too much.

A scout swept into the room, no doubt to see what had caused Kate to shriek.

"Take that thing and get rid of it!" Kate cried out.

"No!" Avery called, but Kate and the scout ignored her.

The scout circled the bird, clearly trying to figure out how to move it without touching it, while Avery hastily considered her options. She could confess everything, follow the scout, or offer to get rid of the bird herself.

Too late. The scout gingerly picked it up by its tail, dropped it into the box with a thud, and disappeared.

Avery's days of communicating with Edward by carrier pigeon were over.

"Honestly," Kate said, still breathless. "You do the strangest things."

Avery didn't respond. For now she had something much more important to do.

chapter 31

Meeting Edith

Avery waited at the agreed-upon spot, pacing and rehearsing what she would say if anyone discovered her plans.

Several minutes passed with no sign of the scout who
was to meet her, until suddenly he appeared, draping some
garments over her arm.

"You have no idea how hard these clothes were to
fetch," he said.

"Thanks," she replied, turning to leave.

"Hey!" he said. "You made a promise!"

Avery stopped, smiled sheepishly, and tossed him a
piece of chocolate she'd stashed in her bedchamber. "Don't
eat it all in one bite."

But the words were barely out of her mouth before the
scout had crammed the chocolate into his mouth, chewing
much louder than necessary.

Avery needed to act before Kate questioned her
absence. She ducked into the shadows and quickly changed

into the outfit—a drab brown dress and a cream apron. She straightened her collar and peeked around the corner to be sure no one would notice. Then she headed into the main tunnel—ducking into alcoves whenever she heard a familiar voice—until she was well beyond the kids' quarters and climbed the stairs that led to the library.

She pressed her ear against the door and, hearing nothing, moved quickly through the empty room and into the kids' stairwell.

✒

Only because of Kendrick's model of the castle did she know which room she needed, and she would get there if it was the last thing she did. Her head swam with a thousand thoughts as she cut through the kitchen where cooks prepared the king's food.

"Stop right there, young lady!" Avery froze. "I don't know you." Avery turned to see Kate's sister wearing the same drab outfit she herself was wearing and holding a butcher knife. She advanced uncomfortably close.

"I'm new to this kitchen," Avery said. "But I know who you are."

The young woman laughed, and Avery was struck again

at how similar her laugh was to Kate's. "You do, eh?" She leaned close to Avery until they were nearly nose to nose. "Then who am I?"

"You're Edith, of course."

"Well!" she said with a look of surprise. "Fine, then. Get back to work."

As soon as she had the chance, Avery bolted, returning to a normal pace only once she reached the hall containing living quarters. She knew from Kendrick's model and room chart that the king's medic lived here, but now all the doors looked alike, and she couldn't just start knocking. One of them was bound to belong to the king. And another to the queen!

She slipped into the shadows to buy time. Truth be told, she should have come with a better plan, but she so badly wanted to help Tuck, she hadn't had time to strategize. And she couldn't ask any of the thirteen-year-olds to help. None would have agreed to this.

Footsteps made Avery turn, and she saw someone coming her direction. Had Edith sent them? No, this someone carried a stack of linens. And she couldn't believe who it was.

"Kate?" She wasn't wearing servants' clothes, but neither

did she bear a star on her wrist. "How did you—?"

Kate put a finger to her lips, joining Avery in the shadows. "When the scouts told me you ran off wearing those clothes, I knew what you were up to. You have no idea where you're going, do you?"

"Not exactly."

Kate dropped the linens. "Follow me."

Avery was grateful for once that Kate knew her way around the castle, but when she marched in the opposite direction, Avery knew they were headed the wrong way. But she couldn't tell Kate. She had promised she would never tell anyone about Kendrick's model.

They walked a long way, eventually taking a stairwell down several floors until they came to a wing of significantly less formal chambers.

The medic doesn't live on this floor.

Kate approached one of the doors and didn't even bother to knock. She just tried the handle, found it unlocked, and shoved it open.

chapter 32

The Mysterious Chamber

Avery followed Kate into an airy space lined with shelves of bottles and where dried plants hung from the ceiling. A breeze swept in from windows where curtains had been swept aside. A threadbare mattress lay in one corner.

After weeks of living in the tunnels, Avery felt a rush of pure delight as she closed her eyes and stood in a room with fresh air. "Where are we?"

"The wise-woman's chamber," Kate said.

Every village had one who met the needs of those too poor to pay what it cost to see a medic—usually a gold coin. Avery assumed the castle's wise-woman was assigned a room down here because she tended the staff and not the king or queen.

Kendrick didn't include this in his room chart. She couldn't wait to tell him about it.

"How did you know where to find her?" Avery asked.

"I just did." Kate moved to the shelves and rummaged

through jars, handing certain ones to Avery. "Rose, lavender, sage, and bay," she said. "And"—Kate moved to another wall—"wormwood, mint, and balm."

"Could the wise-woman come to see Tuck?" Avery asked, trying to manage all the jars.

"No!"

Avery sensed from Kate's tone not to push it. "Do you know what to do with all these?" Noise in the hall made her nervous, but Kate didn't seem concerned.

"Can't be too hard to figure out," Kate said. But she pulled a book from the shelf and thumbed through it then stacked a few more jars atop it and said, "Let's go."

❧

Kate and Avery spent hours into the night in their bedchamber hovered over the jars. Kate furrowed her brow as she scanned the book by candlelight and crushed herbs, mixing the powder into hot tea she'd brought down from the kitchen.

"Don't get your hopes up," Kate said as she ground what smelled like mint. "All of this work may be for nothing."

But of course, it was too late for that. Avery's hopes were as high as they had ever been. "I wish my grandmother could help," Kate added.

"I do, too." Avery cleared her throat. "Speaking of your grandmother. . ."

Kate stopped but didn't look up. "What about her?"

"You said she was responsible for burying the children of royals who died at birth or shortly after."

"Yes."

"Did she bury Queen Elizabeth's son?"

Kate busied herself flipping the pages of the wise-woman's book, but Avery could tell she wasn't actually reading. Finally she whispered, "No."

Presently she shut the book and rose to prepare a steaming mug of something fragrant. "Let's take this to Tuck," Kate said. "If his fever can be broken, this should do it. If it can't, we'll know by morning, and we may need to be prepared to say good-bye."

Avery took the mug and followed Kate out, but she was resolute. Saying good-bye to Tuck was not an option.

At some point, the hard good-byes need to stop. And that time is now.

❧

"Thank you for doing this," Avery said from behind Kate as they walked.

But instead of acknowledging the thanks, Kate slowed and sighed. Avery had to angle beside her to keep the drink from sloshing to the tunnel floor. "What is it, Kate?"

"My grandmother was the castle wise-woman."

"I knew she did more around here than what it seemed."

Kate nodded. "She'd been the wise-woman since Queen Elizabeth's reign. Everything she knew about illness and childbirth and all the rest had been passed down to her through generations of women in her family. Her plan was to teach me next. Then Queen Elizabeth died and everything changed. My grandmother still grew herbs and studied plants, but far less after attending Queen Elizabeth's last childbearing."

So she was at Kendrick's birth!

What if she knew too much about Queen Elizabeth's child? What if someone killed the old woman to keep her silent forever?

The pieces were coming together, but for now Avery hurried on.

For now she needed to concentrate on keeping Tuck alive.

∽∾

Tuck appeared to have shrunk even more, his brow wet, his eyes closed.

Kate lifted his head, and his eyes fluttered open.

Avery explained that they had brought him something to help him get better. He smiled weakly and nodded. Avery carefully put the mug to his lips. When he finished drinking, he lay back and appeared to fall asleep again.

When Kate insisted Avery get some sleep, Avery trudged back to her bed knowing there was nothing more she could do until morning when they would find out if it worked.

Avery heard a noise, and her eyes popped open. She bolted upright. "What are you doing in here?" she said to a girl who sat at the end of her bed.

"Kendrick and Kate asked me to wait for you to wake and then tell you they needed you in Tuck's chamber." The girl cast sad eyes on Avery, and she couldn't bear to hear the girl say the dreaded words.

No! Why did they let me sleep?

The girl left, and Avery stumbled out of bed, dressed, and ran toward the infirmary. Her lungs felt like they might explode as she sprinted.

Please, God, I can't lose anyone else!

She found Tuck's privacy blanket swept aside and a group hovered around his bed. She pushed through them and nearly collapsed at the sight of him.

chapter 33

Living and Dying

Tuck was sitting up and eating from a bowl of broth.

With a smile in his eyes, he said, "My fever has broken," and he patted the chair beside him. "Sit before Kendrick gets back. He kicks everyone out when he visits."

Avery collapsed into the chair, giddy with relief but concerned that Kendrick had risked returning to the infirmary. "He does, does he?"

"Yeah, he thinks I need to be resting all the time."

"He's right," Avery said, noticing that everyone had suddenly left and the blanket had been pulled shut again. Tuck's eyes looked so sunken and his face so thin, she would have to send for rich desserts and jugs of buttermilk. She would take it upon herself to make him well again.

"I need you to know something," Tuck said, laboring to breathe.

"You shouldn't be talking till you get your strength back. Let's do this later."

Tuck reached for her hand. "I'm all right. Listen, you would have made an excellent lady-in-waiting." He paused and she hated knowing it was such an effort just for him to speak, yet he continued. "But I couldn't put you in that kind of danger, and I'm sorry."

Avery shook her head. They didn't have to discuss this—of all things—and certainly not right now. She withdrew her hand and reached for the broth. "Let's just focus on getting you better."

"One more thing," Tuck said, gently pushing the bowl away, and just the way he sounded made dread wash over her. "If I recover. . ."

"Please don't say that. You're already well on the way."

"*If* I recover, I'm going to do whatever is necessary—even if it means risking my life—to get us out of this mess." He waved weakly, as if to indicate everything associated with their captivity.

"But you do that every day, Tuck! You're our leader. We need y—"

"No!" he said, shaking his head. "Being a leader requires doing more for the people I'm trying to lead. Leadership requires self-sacrifice. Hiding down here is no way to live."

"It beats dying," Avery said, forcing a chuckle.

"I agree, but we'll all die if we stay here. That's the joke on the criminals who think they've escaped here. They end up dying anyway because of the contaminated water or the lack of sunshine and all the disease. I won't let it happen to us. I can't let it happen to *you*."

Avery wanted so badly to tell him that she and Kendrick were on the verge of putting the final pieces together and that Kendrick could soon be king. But it was too early, and she had given her word.

Anyway, Tuck looked so energized by his own plans that maybe he needed them to help him get better. Hopefully, his recovery would allow him time to reconsider and see that he didn't need to take any big risks just yet.

"Do we have to have such a serious conversation?" Avery asked.

"Yes, because you need to hear me."

"But you won't make any big decisions while you're still sick, will you?"

"I already have, and I won't be changing my mind."

Guard your heart, she told herself.

Tuck finally took a slurp of soup. He smiled. "It might be easier for you if you got mad at me, maybe even hated me a little."

Avery faked a laugh. "I'll do my best."

Something in the way Tuck looked at her, or maybe it was his willingness to risk his life, made clear what she needed to do. Whether or not he intended to, Tuck had freed her to leave the castle once and for all and reunite with her family.

How long had it been since Edward had told her he would help her if she would meet him in the chapel on the other side of the Salt Sea in five days? Once Tuck had fallen ill, she had lost count as the days became one long, perpetual nightmare. Was it already too late?

"You should rest," Avery said, standing and managing as brave a smile as she could. She helped Tuck set the bowl and spoon aside and settle back down.

When she left, she ran into Kendrick coming the other way.

"How's our boy doing?" he asked.

"Better, I think, but I still say it's dangerous for you to be in there."

"He's long past being contagious, and I'm fine."

"It's your decision," she said with a shrug, but her mind was elsewhere. It was now or never. She could have only a couple of minutes while Kendrick checked on Tuck.

If she acted on this decision, there would be no coming back.

chapter 34

The Light at the End of the Tunnel

Avery cared nothing about seeing Edward again; she lived to get back to her family.

With no idea what Edward wanted in exchange for reuniting her with them, she feared she would have no choice but to accommodate him—within reason. She would not—could not—do anything immoral or illegal. She had been raised better than that. But otherwise, she couldn't imagine anything she would not do.

And once she found her father, she would tell him about all the captive thirteen-year-olds, and he would know what to do.

Not knowing how long she might have before Kendrick returned, Avery slipped into the chamber where he kept his replica of the castle and all his meticulous notes and maps. She riffled through thick stacks of parchment searching, searching. . . .

She knew Kendrick had spent entire nights poring over every passage in the castle's underbelly, seeking potential routes to the country chapel in the event of an emergency. He had plotted every entrance and exit and had boasted recently that he had finally discovered the path.

Finally she came to one map that traced a circuitous route, and all she could do was stop and stare at it in the candlelight. This was the one that held all her hopes and dreams, the one she would put to the test. She carefully folded it and tucked it under her arm. *Thank you, Kendrick!*

Ducking back into the main tunnel, she had no time to lose. For all she knew, she might have already missed Edward. She wouldn't know until she got there.

∽∞∾

Letting hot tears spill, Avery sprinted until her lungs burned. She flew past the kids' chambers and the infirmary. She passed where she had met with Edward and where she had first discovered the crate with the pigeon.

Memories invaded her mind as she ran, and she hated that she might never see her friends again. She knew even as she slowed to check the map that she could be making the worst decision of her life, but *not* taking this chance could be fatal, too.

Whenever Avery began to doubt herself—which was only every few seconds—she reached into her pocket and curled her fingers around Henry's paper boat. That and the ruby necklace beneath her collar were her links to home and constant reminders of her loved ones.

It was time to return to them.

When after at least an hour Avery came to a fork in the tunnel, she skidded to a stop and held Kendrick's map up to the light from a torch on the wall.

The route on his map picked up beyond it, but the direction at the fork was unclear. She had no idea which way she should go.

"Left," a voice whispered.

She spun, but no one was there. *Nerves*, she decided.

But what choice did she have? A disembodied voice, imagined or not, was as good as flipping a coin. Avery hiked up her dress and ran left, the trail of her gown flying behind her.

She ran until she came to sections of the underworld she hadn't known existed. Parts of the tunnel were so narrow the sides brushed her shoulders. Elsewhere the space opened into lofty, vaulted ceilings that reminded her of the upstairs Great Room. Thick rock formations with pointed tips hung from the ceiling like dripping water frozen in time.

She passed disease-ridden people who looked as if they hadn't eaten in weeks, and she saw others who looked like they could crush her with a stare. Who were these castaways with battered bodies and bold eyes, and what cruelties had they inflicted out in the world? What drove them here?

She ran from their cries and taunts with everything she had until she feared she could run no more.

Minutes morphed into hours. Hours felt like days.

Though Avery had to stop running and start walking to conserve her lungs and muscles, the going seemed no easier. The torches on the walls grew fewer and farther between until suddenly there were none and she had to feel her way along. And she quickly deduced why she had to labor so just to keep moving. She was ascending, now ever steeper, climbing, climbing! Was she finally rising from beneath the Salt Sea? Could it be she was nearing the end of this arduous journey?

Finally, at long last, when she had begun to believe darkness could grow no inkier in its blackness, a pinprick of light made her stop and squint then pick up her pace and stare. The light was coming through the edges around a door at the end of the tunnel! A beautiful door surrounded by bright light that portended a gateway to the outside, to freedom!

Soon the eerie, echoing, infernal dripping of the underground began to give way to a sound more pleasant—bells—glorious clanging that signaled some sort of good news. Breathlessly, she rushed for the melody that waxed louder and the light that grew brighter the closer she came.

When finally she came within reach of the door, Avery shoved it open with all her might.

chapter 35

The Wedding

Sunlight, glorious sunlight forced Avery's eyes shut and sent her reeling backward. Shielding her face, she allowed herself to blink once, twice, and finally to let the tree line come into view.

A graceful sloping white spire, so delicate and ethereal she feared it might disappear if she looked away, rose above the tallest trees and came to a razor-sharp tip that pointed almost shyly to the heavens.

The country chapel! The stories were true!

Avery spread her arms wide, as if to embrace the entire landscape.

Despite her exhausting journey, had she not been here on the quest of a lifetime, Avery believed she could have run all the way back to the underbelly of the castle just to tell Kendrick that his map was right—the longest tunnel snaked its way under the Salt Sea all the way to the tiny, beautiful chapel in the village where country girls married.

But in her heart she believed she might never see Kendrick again.

And in the moment she had always anticipated would bring her relief, she felt only sadness at never seeing her friends again. She wished she had found the courage to say good-bye.

∝∞∾

As if in a dream, Avery entered the tiny sanctuary to find that a wedding had just taken place. The bride wore a simple dress and a daisy chain in her raven hair. When she turned, Avery immediately recognized her piercing blue eyes. It was the girl who had led her to Edward in the tunnel.

The groom—laughing in a circle of friends—also turned slowly, and Avery held her breath. Would she know him, too?

He made eye contact and approached her, smiling. Speechless, Avery regretted coming at all. "Glad you could make it," he said. "What a nice surprise."

Finally finding her voice, Avery said, "I thought we were just meeting to talk. To come to some sort of an agreem—"

Edward threw back his head and laughed. "You never

responded to my last message!"

"I didn't read it! The bird was dead! You obviously didn't *expect* me to come."

Edward's face contorted. "Not today, of course. The agreement was for three days ago. It's been eight days since I met you in the tunnel."

Avery's head swam. Time had lost all meaning. "Well, I'm here now, and I risked everything to get here. So tell me where my family is."

"Oh, I wish I could," he said with a smile that exuded false sympathy. "But Avery, we had a deal." And he turned to walk away.

"No!" she blurted. "You can't let me come all this way and then just decide not to tell me where they are!" Several guests had stopped chatting and were now watching.

He stopped and turned back, his smile gone. "I just did."

Avery closed the distance between them and came face-to-face with him until their noses nearly touched. "How did you get Henry's boat?"

Edward put a hand on her arm, squeezing hard. He spoke softly, in measured tones. "I don't owe you any information, but let me tell you something that could save your life, because I still consider you a friend—despite how you're acting *at my wedding*: don't return to the castle."

Pulling back, she studied his face, trying to comprehend. She did feel bad about causing a scene here, now. Trying her best to sound civil, she said, "Just tell me why."

Edward glanced both ways, and people looked away. "Look carefully at the guests," he whispered.

Avery looked past him and noticed that the simply dressed congregants, talking and smiling in clusters, were young. On closer examination she realized they were all the missing thirteen-year-olds! Alive!

She closed her eyes and shook her head as he lightened his grip on her arm. "How did they get here? *Why* are they here?"

"Let's just say we're organized, and the king is about to be dethroned. It would have happened the day of the race had you let Thomas win."

Avery let the words sink in. "Thomas would have assassinated the king during his private audience," she whispered.

"You're catching on."

A cold, hard look overtook Edward, and suddenly everything became clear to Avery. "You've built an army! *You* snatched everyone from the castle. *This* is the secret mission you kept referring to, the one you wanted my help with. You wanted me to meet you here so I could be part of your legion. Do you even know where my family is? Did you ever?"

Edward let go of her and smiled. "Listen, Avery, this may look like a wedding, but it's not. It's a call to arms. Everyone here knew that. And now so do you."

"Smart," Avery said, nodding. "Use my family to draw me here. Find one of the paper boats in my brother's room and make me think you got it from him so I'd believe you could take me to him and my father. Gotta hand it to you."

Edward pressed his lips together and cocked his head. "Guilty," he said, "but here you are, and here we are. And your best—and probably only—chance to find your family is to join the resistance."

"You really believe the end justifies the means," she said, shaking her head. "Good-bye, Edward."

"Last chance, Avery!" he called after her as she strode toward the door. "Join us as we take back the throne or die in the tunnels!"

Avery turned. "The *king* isn't our problem. Kill him and we could be in worse trouble than we are now. Not to mention, you could be hanged for treason!"

"Don't say you haven't been warned. And you should know that if the entire castle needs to be destroyed in order to kill the king, we're prepared to do that."

"You wouldn't! Your sister could be locked in the Tower right now."

"Is that so?" Edward nodded over his shoulder, and Avery followed his gaze to where a nicely dressed Ilsa stood chatting in a group. "Who do you think started the fire?"

Is there no limit to what these two might do?

"You, too, could disappear without a trace, Avery. Stay with us and let your friends think something tragic happened to you."

She shook her head. With the entire castle in jeopardy, Avery knew what she had to do.

Edward said, "Be careful. Tell anyone what you know and that paper boat will be the last thing you ever see of your family."

Avery slipped out of the chapel and raced to the door of the tunnel that led back to her friends. She would never stop trying to reach her family, but it was time to warn the king.

chapter 36

A Friendship Uncovered

Somehow the journey back took longer. Why did that always seem so?

Avery returned to Tuck's sick chamber—winded and anxious.

"Where were you?" Kate whispered, rising from the stool beside Tuck's bed—where he lay sleeping.

Avery shrugged. "I needed time to think."

The look in Kate's eyes told Avery she knew there was something more.

Kate didn't press, and Avery didn't offer.

In the days following, Avery took a book to the infirmary each time she took her turn on the stool beside Tuck's bed. Some days she read to him, and other days she asked him to tell her stories from his childhood. She sensed he enjoyed their time together as much as she did. Nearly every day when she arrived, he was deep in conversation with Kendrick.

But then one morning at breakfast, Tuck appeared in the doorway, and the dining room burst into applause. Everyone moved to clear a spot and find him a plate.

Avery had to fight the urge to cry as she watched Tuck sit in his usual spot. And as if he couldn't manage it himself, kids helped fill his plate and pour his drink and push his chair closer to the table. They did everything for him except spoon the food into his mouth.

Avery smiled at the frustration on his face. They were one step closer to getting the old Tuck back.

Of course, this also meant they were one step closer to learning what Tuck planned to do next. Avery was certain she wasn't ready to hear it.

∞

Kendrick invited Avery to join him where he kept his castle replica and said, "The strangest thing happened. One of my maps—this one—went missing, but it was returned the next day. You know how neatly I like to keep them, but you can see it has been folded. Any idea who might have borrowed it?"

Avery wondered if Kendrick could hear her heartbeat the way she did. She was certain she was blushing from her neck to her hairline.

"I'm sure whoever it was had a good reason," she said, trying to sound casual but knowing she sounded anything but.

"No doubt."

"And I'm sure she—or he—would love to tell you what happened but doesn't feel like she—or he—should."

Kendrick set down the map and smoothed it out. He sat back and looked her in the eyes. "When you're ready to tell me where you went and why you've been so quiet since you returned, I'm ready to listen. I hope by now you know we're friends."

Avery looked down then nodded. Lying never solved anything. She began cautiously. "Edward asked me to meet him in the chapel."

"Ilsa's brother? I thought he was—"

"He's back."

"And you're telling me my map was accurate? It took you to the chapel?"

Avery nodded. "It was perfect, except—"

"Except you had to guess at the fork."

"Right. I went left."

"And it worked? You didn't have to double back?"

"No, left was correct."

Kendrick grabbed a quill and filled in that portion of his map, asking, "So what did Edward want?"

Avery bit her lip, considered Edward's threat, and decided it was a risk she had to take. If she didn't tell Kendrick, she'd put her friends at risk. If she told Kendrick the truth, she put her family at risk. She moved to stand close to Kendrick so she could whisper the words—

"He's planning to destroy the king."

She expected Kendrick to doubt her or at least criticize her for meeting him, but he merely nodded. "I know."

"You do? How?"

"Why do you think I tried so hard to map the route to the chapel? We need a way of escape. A war is coming. I don't know when or with whom, but if we stay here, we'll end up fighting for our lives."

"Then I'm right that it's time to talk to the king," Avery said.

Kendrick blew out a long breath. "I think you might be."

❧

Kate unrolled a thick canvas onto Avery's mattress. "I've discovered how your mother knew so much about life within the castle."

Avery stood shoulder to shoulder with her, peering at a painting of Queen Elizabeth in a velvet chair surrounded by beautiful ladies. It had been commissioned around the same time—if not the same day—as the other painting Avery had discovered in the storage room on the kids' side of the castle. Avery could tell because the setting, backdrop, and style were the same.

The portrait featured the queen's smooth skin and exotic mismatched eyes. One of the ladies behind her had light hair and a radiant smile, clearly muted by the painter, probably in an attempt not to detract from the queen.

"My mother!" Avery said, gasping. She ran her fingers over the canvas, marveling at the image of this younger version of the woman she had known, but made up, and with her hair done up, and dressed as Avery had never seen—in castle finery.

"From what I've been able to uncover," Kate said, "she was a lady-in-waiting, a fixture at court. I hope this answers some of your questions."

"Hardly," Avery whispered, unable to tear her eyes away. She was dying to know how Kate knew this woman was her mother, but that question could wait. "May I keep this?"

"For a day or two. I need to return it before anyone knows it's missing."

⤫

Avery accepted Kendrick's help pulling her up onto the sloping rooftop with the painting under her arm. She unrolled it and held it before him. "That's my mother," she said, pointing. "Can you believe it?"

Kendrick's face was blank.

"What is it?" Avery asked.

"I knew her."

Avery rerolled the canvas and set it on her lap. "What are you saying?"

"The lady in that painting was a friend of the woman who raised me. She was the one I told you about who was talking to the woman who cared for me the day I learned of my connection to the king. Avery, if that's who you say it is, your mother knew who I was."

"That can't be possible."

"She often visited us."

"No," Avery said, but she knew Kendrick had no reason to lie. "It can't be a coincidence that our mothers were friends. Maybe I'm here *because* my mother knew the truth about you."

"Maybe you're part of the secret," Kendrick said.

But Avery wasn't ready to even consider what that might imply.

chapter 37

Tuck's Announcement

Avery sat with Tuck in the tunnel Great Room where their friends gathered to read or talk. The rest looked as weary as she felt. Months of dark, cold underground living had taken their toll.

"I need to talk about the ring," she said, unable to look in his eyes.

"Ring?"

Avery considered dropping it. If Tuck had forgotten about the ring or never intended to return it, she didn't want to make things awkward between them. And yet he was getting better, and she wanted their friendship fully restored.

"On Christmas Day you gave me a gold ring shaped like a crown with small pointed spikes."

Tuck smiled, and Avery knew he hadn't forgotten. She held out her hand. His pause told her she wasn't likely to get it back.

"Tonight I plan to make an announcement," he said quietly. "You'll want to hear it, because I suspect you won't want the ring anymore."

∞

At midnight court, the chatter was upbeat, but Avery felt only a pit in her stomach as she took her seat at the front beside Tuck's chair. She wished she could enjoy getting back to normalcy when Kendrick and Kate took their seats and Tuck entered to the greetings of the rest of the thirteen-year-olds.

Though tonight he would sit rather than stand, it was still great to have him back. He looked as nervous as he had the day he announced Ilsa would be the nominee for lady-in-waiting.

He called for order and dived right in. "No more halfhearted efforts," he said. "We must overturn every stone to find the missing friends and brothers and sisters among us. Already scouts are doing everything they can."

Avery shot a glance at Kendrick as Tuck continued. "We've employed residents of the underworld to see what they can uncover on the streets. Thanks to Kendrick's efforts, we are scouring the castle—room by room—until we exhaust every nook and cranny. And yet there is one place we have not looked."

Scanning the room, Avery could tell she was not the only one on the edge of her seat.

Tuck licked his lips and glanced at the floor. "Tomorrow I set sail for the Forbidden City, our last hope to end our captivity."

No clapping, no hugging, no shouts of praise. The kids sat wide-eyed and slack-jawed. Avery assumed they were all thinking what she was.

After tomorrow we likely won't ever see him again.

He needs to know the truth about Kendrick's identity.

∞

Kendrick was waiting for her in an alcove off the dining room.

"Tuck can't travel!" Avery blurted before he had a chance to open his mouth. "He's barely well enough to be out of bed, let alone sail on the Salt Sea! Either you tell him the truth tonight or I will!"

Kendrick shook his head. "I don't want him to go either, but I can't tell him who I am just to keep him here. I haven't told *anyone.*"

"You told *me*!"

"No, Avery. You figured it out. I wouldn't have told you, either."

Though his comment cut deep, Avery steeled herself against taking it personally. She paced. "We can't let him even get in a boat. *Think* of something."

"Why? What if he's right? What if he finds something in the Forbidden City that can help? Give me one reason he shouldn't try."

Avery stopped. "Because I love him!"

The words were out before she could stop them or explain.

"Oh," Kendrick said, his eyes widening. He dropped into a chair, staring, a hand on each knee.

Avery wished she could crawl into a hole.

Finally Kendrick stood and adjusted his glasses. "I might have a solution."

∞

Finally desperate enough to do what she should have done in the beginning, Avery sneaked upstairs to the castle chapel with its stunning gold-gilded walls and stained-glass windows. How many times had her mother told her, *"You will find the answers to your most important questions there"*?

She sighed with relief at being alone in the tiny, familiar space. Shaky with pent-up emotion, she glided down the center aisle and knelt at the altar the way her mother had at the humble chapel back home.

She poured out her heart to God, again the way she had heard her mother do. She asked for wisdom, for safety for her family, and she begged the Lord not to let Tuck get in that boat.

At the end of her prayer, she lay on the crimson carpet and stared at the ceiling where famous royals were painted in vivid color. Castle lore said the impressive mural represented the kingdom's darkest stories.

Figures in black capes danced through the scenes, swords extended, while figures in white—presumably innocent royals—fell backward, pools of red at their feet.

Avery wished the famous figures could talk.

She scanned the faces for Queen Elizabeth and had to smile at how the painter accentuated her brown and blue eyes, much too wide for her delicate face. A halo hovered above her.

More exhausted than she knew, Avery soon fell asleep, the kingdom's heroes pirouetting back to life in her dreams.

chapter 38

The Painting

When morning broke and the stained-glass windows allowed shards of dancing sunlight to reach Avery's eyes, she awoke with a start.

Instantly, she knew three things with certainty:

Under no circumstances would she allow Tuck to set sail for the Forbidden City today.

She would regret sleeping on the chapel's hard floor all night—no doubt suffering a well-earned backache the rest of the day.

And the council—specifically Kate—would be hot with anger that she had been gone all night. This time, Avery deserved it.

She lay staring at the ceiling, trying to conjure a plausible excuse.

And she saw it for the first time. Sitting up, she looked closer at Queen Elizabeth in the mural.

In a cold sweat, Avery struggled to her feet and climbed

up onto one of the wooden pews where she stood and stared even more closely, stunned she hadn't noticed before.

The best-kept secrets are often hidden right before our eyes.

She had so focused on the queen's eyes that she had missed the most remarkable detail.

Queen Elizabeth held *two* babies.

∘⧜∘

Avery raced back, hoping to talk to Kendrick. History said nothing about two royal children from the king and his first queen. What if the other child also lived?

She reached her room, where Kate sat with her back to the doorway, with that regal posture and porcelain skin, carefully pinning her hair. Was it possible Avery's friend was so acquainted with the castle and its ways because she herself had royal blood?

Kate had withheld details about her own sister. *"There are things you don't know about me, and it's better this way."*

Avery's mind raced, but she would not talk to Kate about the chapel ceiling until she spoke to Kendrick.

"News!" a scout shouted, running through the tunnels, and Kate turned too quickly for Avery to avoid being seen.

"Don't you move," Kate said, as she scurried out with

everyone else to hear what the scout had to say. "You've got a lot of explaining to do. I was worried sick!"

The scout continued shouting, "News!" until everyone had gathered, then he said, "For the first time in weeks, the king is emerging from his bedchamber, and word is he has an announcement that will change the course of history!" Over the cacophony of the response, he hollered, "And Tuck has called a meeting of the council in the dining room!"

⸎

Moments later, Avery made eye contact with Tuck, as eager to block his travel plans as Kate likely was to chastise her for the night before, but now was not the time.

"The king is to make the announcement within the hour," Kendrick said. "The court is filling with dignitaries, and the commons outside are bursting with people. This is going to be big, and not even his closest advisers seem to know what he's going to say."

"We need to get upstairs to a grate," Kate said, and all eyes turned to Tuck.

"Will you be able to make it?" Avery asked.

"Are you kidding? I wouldn't miss it for anything!"

Avery, with Tuck on one side and Kate and Kendrick on the other, looked down on the Great Hall as the court filled with familiar faces. Anyone who was anyone was there. Hordes stood shoulder to shoulder like cattle.

"What do you think he's going to say?" Avery whispered.

"No idea," Kendrick said. "I thought the next announcement from the throne would be about his death."

Queen Angelina entered in a beautiful white gown with gold sleeves. Her high headdress was made of gold and pearls. Not since her wedding had she looked so magnificent.

"No sign of black," Kate said. "So apparently no mourning."

"Maybe," Tuck said, "this will just be about his miraculous recovery—like mine. See the scribes in the wings? Whatever it is, it'll be spread throughout the realm by noon."

Avery could feel the tension rising.

A quartet of trumpets sounded, and the king suddenly appeared. He was pale and frail and leaned on his cane, but he advanced to the raised dais unaided and ascended to his throne.

The room grew eerily silent in anticipation of his words.

chapter 39

Life and Death

Gone was the king's regal bearing, his air of utter power. In its place sat a shriveled, ancient monarch like a child in an oversized chair.

He spoke so quietly, the room hushed and the crowd leaned forward to catch his words.

"The rumors are true," he said. "I am dying."

The audience gasped. Kings, after all, never admitted to mortality.

He held up a hand for silence. "But that is not why I appear before you today. I come with good news." He motioned for Angelina to join him. The queen rose from her great chair, a smile slowly growing. In her dazzling gown, she glided to the far side of his throne and gently laid her hand on his bony shoulder.

As he gazed up at her and she down at him, he cleared his throat and seemed to muster enough strength to be heard more clearly. "It gives me great pleasure to announce that my beloved queen is with child, and I am confident it is a boy! We have an heir!"

The court erupted in cheers and thunderous applause, and within seconds the word must have reached outside, for a second wave of raucous cheering sounded.

Avery darted a glance at Kendrick even as bells pealed in the distance. *Had the people responded this way at the announcement of* his *coming?*

The king appeared to want to say more, perhaps a word of thanks or farewell, but there was no quieting the crowd. Shouts of congratulations, laughing, crying, embracing, singing, dancing, the playing of instruments all drowned out any more official components of the festivities.

"Apparently they've forgotten he's dying," Tuck said. "Look at him."

The king looked as weary as Avery had ever seen him, and she wondered if he would be able to exit as he had entered. Even Angelina actually looked concerned for him, but that was likely for appearances.

"How can he be sure she's carrying a boy?" Avery whispered.

Kate scoffed. "Kings are always sure. Who's going to tell him he's wrong?"

"Only a medic when a daughter is born," Avery said.

"If *she's* convinced her baby is a boy, the king is as good as dead."

"Who but we can save him?" Avery asked. "And how?"

"Warn him in a letter?" Kendrick suggested.

Tuck shrugged. "Or one of us disguises ourselves as an adult and requests a private audience."

Avery looked to Kate for her idea. "We'd better get back," she said. "I'd like to hear where you were all night."

It wasn't lost on Avery that Kate had offered no idea, but she also wanted to end the drama about her absence, so she decided to defuse Kate with the truth. "I needed a little time alone in the chapel, and I fell asleep."

"Did you learn anything while you were there?" Kendrick asked.

Avery didn't miss the way he held her gaze. *Does he know what I discovered?*

Below, Avery noticed scouts squirreling away meats intended for the celebrants that would be enjoyed by enthusiastic kids waiting in the tunnels for news. They would be thrilled to hear of the future prince, Avery thought, unaware of the prince living among them.

As Kate and Avery headed back together, Kate said,

"We'd better prepare for the transition of power."

Avery shook her head. "No! We must get to the king quickly and tell him the truth!"

Kate gave her a disgusted look. "Honestly, Avery. At some point you will realize that you cannot be everyone's savior."

The words came out of Avery's mouth before she could stop them—

"And at some point, you will need to tell me the truth about whose side you are on."

∞

Avery desperately wanted to get alone with Kendrick and ask him about the painting of Queen Elizabeth with the two babies and also what he really thought of the news. With Angelina carrying the king's heir, was Kendrick's life in less jeopardy or more?

Avery looked around the lunch table for him and was about to go search for him when Tuck appeared and motioned for her to join him.

Avery smiled until she saw the look on his face and froze. He still looked resolute about his plans. She had hoped the king's announcement might distract or detain him.

With all that had gone on, she had again lost track of time. Lunch had been delayed, and late afternoon was approaching. Tuck had said nothing of changing his mind about leaving for the Forbidden City. If she could not stop him, she would likely say good-bye to him tonight for the last time.

Her stomach twisted as she approached him.

"I've prepared a boat," he said quietly when they were alone. "One of the scouts found an outlet that opens directly to the Salt Sea."

"You don't have to do this," Avery said. "If you're trying to prove your usefulness, don't. You're needed here."

Tuck shook his head. "I'm not trying to prove anything. I believe going to the Forbidden City is the right thing to do, and I need you to believe it, too."

"But I don't! You might never come back."

Tuck nodded. "I know that, but I also believe it's better to die attempting a good thing than to live doing nothing."

That was certainly not what she wanted to hear, noble as it was. "So take me with you," Avery said. "I'll help you."

Tuck smiled. "You know I can't do that."

A sob rose in Avery's throat, but before she could respond, he added, "I need something from my room.

Will you wait here?"

Avery nodded, suspecting he was going to fetch the crown ring to leave her as a gift to remember him by. She needed to think of a way to stall him—and fast.

chapter 40

Farewell

Avery waited in agony in the main tunnel as kids came and went, celebrating the king's announcement. What was taking Tuck so long just to find a ring?

But when she saw a shadow move quickly down the hall in the opposite direction, she squinted, realizing it was Tuck.

He's leaving!

She hiked up her dress and took off after him, yelling, but was drowned out by the noise of the celebration. Either because of her desperation or because he was still weak, she gained on Tuck, the smell of the sea stronger with every step.

She caught him as they reached a door that led to moss-covered stairs carved into a jetty that stretched into the water.

"Stop!" she hollered, grabbing his arm, tears stinging her eyes. "How dare you leave without saying good-bye— to *me*, of all people? Do I really mean so little to you after all this time?"

Tuck, also panting, shook his head, pointing.

Out in the foaming water, the boat was slowly moving out to sea, its young pilot a dark figure silhouetted in the moonlight.

"Kendrick?" she called. "Come back!"

Kendrick waved a slow farewell.

Terror gripped her as the rightful heir to the throne headed toward the Forbidden City. If anyone else knew who Kendrick was, he would be a dead man for sure.

"So many unanswered questions," she whispered.

Tuck looked at her, confusion on his face.

Avery and Tuck stood watching until the boat became but a tiny dot on the horizon. Then, long after the rest of the thirteen-year-olds had disbanded for the night, they sat together at the dining table carrying heavy, wordless burdens. They hadn't even told Kate that Kendrick was gone.

"What do we do now?" Tuck asked.

It was time she told him the truth. "Would you meet me in the chapel after breakfast tomorrow morning? I need to show you something that will explain everything."

Tuck nodded.

"You had better come alone."

Avery skipped breakfast to arrive in the chapel early to pray for Kendrick and prepare for Tuck.

In addition to the light pouring through the stained-glass windows, she was puzzled to find the chapel lit by clusters of fat white candles, giving the sanctuary a warm, hazy glow and producing a wreath of incense that made her eyes burn.

Avery soon realized she was not alone.

An old man knelt at the altar the way her mother had back home. She'd not seen an adult pray here and was about to leave him when she noticed his cane. And then his coat. Slowly it dawned on her.

This wasn't just any old man. Avery had walked in on her dying king!

He had come to pray for what? There were so many options.

She knew she should turn and leave, but she couldn't shake one thought—

Do I stay and risk my life to tell him the truth, or do I risk everything and everyone else by leaving?

Everything her mother and father had ever taught her

came pouring back, and she took one terrifying step.

Her feet felt like lead, but for good or bad, this was her moment.

And Avery was going to seize it.

About the Authors

Trisha White Priebe is a wife, mom, writer, editor, and shameless water polo enthusiast. She advocates for orphans, speaks at retreats, and enjoys assisting her husband in ministry. She wrote *Trust, Hope, Pray: Encouragement for the Task of Waiting* and *A Sherlock Holmes Devotional: Uncovering the Mysteries of God.* She blogs at RescuingSunday.com.

Jerry B. Jenkins, former vice president for publishing at the Moody Bible Institute of Chicago and currently a member of its board of trustees, is the author of more than 185 books, including the bestselling Left Behind series. He teaches writers at JerryJenkins.com.

coming April 2017

The Paper Boat

The king is not well and is in a hurry to hand over his power to a new generation when rumors begin to circulate through the kingdom. It appears the king is unaware of the sinister plot against the orphans and that it is the doing of the queen, who wants to be sure her child is heir to the throne.

As Avery weighs the pros and cons of seeking an audience with the king, the castle is dealt a heavy blow; but Avery decides the risk is worth taking, and she steps out of the shadows for the first time since entering the castle.

When Avery is offered an opportunity of a lifetime, will she choose a life free from hardship within the castle walls. . .or her family and the home she left behind?

Don't miss this exciting conclusion!

Discover this and more books from Shiloh Run Press
at your favorite bookstore or at www.shilohrunpress.com.